MAY   2011

FR(9)

LAUGH NOW

Rahiem Brooks

Prodigy Publishing Group
PHILADELPHIA

The characters and events in this book are fictitious. Any similarity to real persons, living or dead is coincidental and not intended by the author.

All rights reserved. Published in the United States by Prodigy Publishing Group a division of the CHRISTINA LUNDIN GROUP
www.prodigypublishinggroup.com

Cover design by: Stephen Richards. stephenrichardsdesign@gmail.com
Author Photo by: Matt Kern. Mkern728@gmail.com

Cataloging-in-Publication Data is on file with the Library of Congress.

ISBN 978-0-578-05777-4

Library of Congress Catalog Card Number: 2010928322

PRINTED IN THE UNITED STATES OF AMERICA

First Editon trade paperback edition: September 2010

FOR NYOKA AND DONNA

My favorite, and only, two aunts, for their undying encouragement to excel and pursue greatness.

ACKNOWLEDGMENTS

No author is an island; however, I am a peninsula. Only a certain stock of men and women know what it truly took to bring this book to my readers.

Mom and dad, what can I say, but thanks for it all from conception.

Mary Arthur, can't wait to start another one, just to read to you over coffee and cake.

Beverly Rickenbacher, Nyoka Presley, Donna Saunders, Rhonesia Brooks, Marcus Gary Kevin Woodard, Onte McClendon, Peter Weschler, Ronnie Williams & Nathan Anderson, you all know the support that you offered to bring this book to life, and I am forever grateful. Thanks!

Stephen Richards, thanks for assuring that my novel screamed for attention on store's shelves. Matthew Kern thanks for the headshots and video, you're the best.

Thanks, Khumbulani Coomz Ngangelizwe, Marian Avila, Walter Vickerie, Tai'Kwan Cureton, George Mensah, Brandi "Bonnie Lookingfor Clyde" Lyons, Terry Jones & Federico Patchico Ojano my Face Book friends that allowed me to E-mail an excerpt of my manuscript to you, before I ever mentioned my book on FB.

Al-Saadiq Banks good lookin' for E-mailing me while I was on lock with information to help me finish this novel; and, thanks for the Face Book inbox messages that helped me bring this book to fruition.

Lastly, I thank Antoine Robinson, Benjamin Shelton, Andre Henry, Anthony Randall, Ali Riley, Daniel Charles & Alain Gilles, my gangsters on lock that read, critiqued, and helped revise my material as I developed it during my days behind the wall. None of them more valuable than Keith Stephens, who read every handwritten page as I wrote them, and kept me full of coffee and cappuccino to get through the night writing, so that he could read the following day, and comment on every sentence.

LAUGH

NOW

PART ONE

DECEMBER 2002

CHAPTER 1

The weight that crushed BG's shoulders had been lifted when Dre agreed to accompany him from a serene suburb to the hostile ghetto-ness of North Philadelphia. Dre snaked a black Dodge Charger along I-76, rattling to the baseline of the Jada Kiss *Why* single. BG rode shotgun, seat reclined like a boss, and he breathed somewhat normally— white boys needed balls to cop down the infamous J Street. Brent Gower, at seventeen had earned the moniker BG, and he had balls the size of Russia. Dre glanced at the Girard Avenue ramp, and BG stole a glance at the young thug, just four years removed from the ghetto where they were headed.

Andre Bezel had smoothly transitioned into suburbia, and was the Upper Merion High School all-American running back. He conspired with BG, the quarterback, on the football turf. And they drove to a notorious drug turf to further that conspiracy. Dre was not a member of BG's gang, reserved for the toughest white boys in King of Prussia; that was beneath him. Dre's blackness and he being a product of the hostile North Philadelphia streets was a grand reason for BG to use him. Dre's father, James "Dope" Bezel was serving a life sentence for a crack conspiracy, which made room for a lame to sweep Dre's mother off her feet and into King of Prussia. That did not arrest Dre from being intimately connected to the streets, with a Rolodex of connections left behind by his father.

At the off-ramp light, Dre turned left onto Girard Avenue at 35th Street. He drove pass the Philadelphia Zoo, crossed the Girard Avenue Bridge, over the Schuylkill River— which separated West Philadelphia from north, Dre's side of town. Dre mentally relived ghetto gospel and news headlines that confirmed what a zoo the 15-square miles of North Philadelphia was. Dre meandered along the SEPTA number-15 trolley tracks. The street numbers dropped traffic light by traffic light; that pay day for the trip coming.

33rd Street. Fairmount Park.
29th Street. Blue Jay Diner.
25th Street. Girard College.
21st Street. Berean Institute.
17th Street. St. Joseph Prep School.
16th Street. St Joseph Hospital.

Dre flipped a left up 16th Street. The streets, buildings and houses became scruffier. The teens stared at the crude neighborhood, both glad that they lived where they had. It was not always that way for Dre, though. He had to get used to his new home in the suburbs. Dre pulled up at 16th and Jefferson Streets, and BG did not believe his eyes. The sight was a first; his drugs were usually delivered. The street had three occupied houses with rent paying tenants; the rest were home to squatters. Many other houses were boarded up. A few empty spots where homes had burned down, had housed abandoned vehicles. Young hoodlums loitered on the corner, without a thought of school the following day.

Winos drank joyously around a barrel that burned wood in an attempt to ward off sinister winds.

Three black males in a Crown Vic on spinners, pulled behind the Charger. Through the rearview mirror, Dre watched the thugs and put his Desert Eagle on his lap. He knew from experience that the 17th Street sentries drove lemons. A car carrying priests was deemed a threat in that ghetto. Equally, a car with a black and white boy—like Dre and BG—in it was registered as two squares in town to cop, and be robbed afterward.

Dre killed the engine and heard a boom box that played *99 Problems* by Jay Z very loudly after midnight. Only in a ghetto was that possible. BG opened the car door and stepped out.

"I'm staying here." Dre confirmed.

"Good ol' Goldie here will be by my side," BG said, and showed Dre, Goldie, the .45-cal that he had in his waist. "I know that she's a ride or die bitch." BG ignored the feeling in his gut that screamed for him to get the hell out of there.

"Remember, I told you not to do this." Dre had tried to convince BG to give him the money and let him cop for him, for a fee, but BG wasn't having that.

BG grabbed his Woolrich winter coat and walked away from the Charger. He was not for Dre's negative energy. He was about that paper. Period! BG crossed 16th Street and walked up Jefferson toward 17th. A pair of eyes from a second story window followed him step by step. BG walked, shivering in the freezing air, toward the hustlers on the corner. He paused in the middle of the notorious drug zone, reached in his jeans for a slip of paper on which he had Trigger's number. He ripped his Nextel from the clip, flipped it open and began to dial.

Interrupting his call, a tall thug dressed in all black, stepped out of an alley and put a snub nosed .38 on BG's temple. Another lanky, thuggish-looking kid snatched the cell phone and told BG, "You don't need this shit," before he slammed the phone shut and put it his own pocket.

"This either," a third man said, and grabbed Goldie from BG's waist.

With BG stripped of his security, his worst nightmare became a reality, right there on the block. BG felt embarrassed and lost. His heart raced with fear. His mind swirled with Dre's discouraging comment, *Remember, I told you not to do this.* He was frisked quickly, but the search seemed in slow motion. The robber with the .38 demanded to know where the money was hidden. BG acted dumb founded and the skinny kid swiftly raised Goldie into the air. Goldie had blacked BG's eye in one motion.

The kid said, "Maybe that will help your memory?"

BG mopped blood from his face, as it coldly trickled and began to freeze. He had the message. Through clinched teeth, BG told the robbers that the money was hidden in his Timberland boots. He kicked them off and the men searched them. They found the $5,000 stash and then the beefy man threw BG. He landed hard on the front of a Camry, scrambled to his feet quickly—a gift from playing football—and ran back to the Charger.

Blood continued to rain from BG's face as he hopped into the car. Dre peeled off, tires screaming under the powerful acceleration.

"What the fuck happened back there?" Inside Dre laughed hysterically. He loved when the plan came together. Especially his plans.

CHAPTER 2

\ *The next day, Kareem Bezel, an authentic intellect and undoubtedly Upper Merion High's most savants,* strolled out of the debate team meeting. He made his way to the school lobby on a mission. He had always been known for his friendliness, but his popularity skyrocketed when classmates and teachers discovered that he was a child prodigy. At sixteen-years-old, he was a senior at Upper Merion and a highly regarded, quick witted student, and very likely to succeed. How he managed being a distinguished honor roll student, the most stylish boy on campus, and a class clown baffled many.

Kareem reached the lobby, and called Express Limo on his cell phone. He put on his older white man fake voice and told the receptionist that he was John Carter. Not Kareem, or even his nick name, Reem. After the formalities, he requested a sedan be delivered to the school with a driver to pick up his son. Kareem smiled; he was the son, and the father. A sexy smile, complimented by plush lips that women adored. He had a sleek, natural Caribbean tan, which shone bright under the black that he wore. He had perfect African features: slim head, snout, and expertly chiseled from track and field and weight lifting. He was only 5'6" and very slender. His favorite adage was: Big things came in small packages. And he had a bombshell in the package for the limo service: and, not of the Naomi Campbell persuasion.

He was clueless as to who John Carter was. And didn't care. For that day's purpose, he was poignantly another one of his credit card fraud victims. Kareem had been rewarded with Mr. Carter's American Express card during one of his many "mailbox shopping" sprees. He was amazed at what he found in mailboxes that were not his own. The receptionist recorded John Carter's credit card number and then informed him that the company only had limos available.

"Okay, what is your hourly rate, for the limo service?" Kareem asked, despite knowing the answer.

"That depends on the vehicle," she told him. "We have Lincoln, Cadillac, Jaguar, and Hummer."

"The Jaguar will be great," Kareem confirmed, like a true businessman. He wanted to enjoy the sleekness of the luxury ride. He had business to tend to and a limo lent credibility to his up-coming plan.

"Right now, we have the Jaguar S-type 4.0 at $325 for the first hour, and $105 each additional hour."

Kareem muffled the phone and pretended to clear his throat uncontrollably. "You can go ahead and charge the card for two hours. Thank you."

Kareem patiently waited having done that so many times with different limousine services. On occasion, even if he had no use for the limo, he would rent a limo to activate a credit card. Most other crafty men—well, amateurs—used gas station self service pumps to try and activate a card.

Not Kareem.

He had learned that creditors flagged accounts that had a gas pump as the first transaction. Kareem was young, but he had learned early—at fifteen—that when the water department threatened to terminate service, one had to find a creative way to stop that. He received his confirmation from the limo service, and watched his older brother, Dre stroll off the football field.

CHAPTER 3

The air blew hard and whistled a fine tune as Dre walked off the football field. He watched a limo pull off, and thought, *I hate these rich pussies.* His quads were cramped and made practice intolerable, so he cut out early. Besides, why should he practice, if the quarterback was not?

Coach Cramer was disgusted by his star running back's faux complaints and barked, "Shape up, Bezel, or be shipped out!"

Who the fuck does he think he's kidding? Dre thought as he paced across the school grounds. He was unfazed by the ultimatum. Five-feet-ten and solid 170-pounds, Dre was the districts only recognized all-American. Local media and alumni idolized his cocoa complexion, wavy hair, dark brown eyes, and sly grin, which he showcased each time that he made a big play in a game. He was the school's touch down record holder, and dubbed *Dre Bezel the Great.* And the coach was not shipping any damn body out.

He entered the locker room, with its characteristic smell of stinking sweat and Lysol. He sat on a wood bench, kicked off his cleats, and pulled off his tights and jersey. He exposed an overdeveloped physique that screamed ex-convict. Ladies, both young and old, adored his sculptured body, which was why he dated the head cheerleader.

Dre reached into his locker to fetch a towel when in his peripheral, he observed BG approached him. Dre jumped to his feet defensively, and thought, *this cat had to be crazy to think that he caught me slipping.* He hated BG, as did most of the students at the school. In fact, most people in that suburb nestled fifteen miles away from Philadelphia, could not stomach BG off the football field. He had mentally controlled many impressionable minds; Andre Bezel's was not one of them, contrary to BG's belief.

When BG was in arms reach, Dre, with cobra-like speed, grabbed BG with both hands and choke-slammed him hard against a wall of lockers. He proved his company was unwanted.

BG tried to speak, but Dre was not having that.

"Look—Brent," Dre said, insulting BG by calling him his birth name. No one did that. Breathing hard in his face, Dre continued, "All I want to do is play ball and get out of here. I didn't set you up, and warned you not to go down there. I'm telling you, stop the fuck running around spreading shit about me."

Avery Snobli, BG's second-in-command stepped toward Dre.

Dre tightened both of his hands around BG's throat as he spat, "Tell your little fuck boy to back off, or I'll break your fucking neck."

BG quickly held up his hand, waving Avery off. BG was aware that the Bezel brothers took Judo, and that Dre was very capable of carrying out the threat. BG did not desire to find out. Avery backed off and then Dre tossed BG toward him and they both stumbled.

"Dre, you have it all fucked up. I come in peace." BG pleaded, massaging his throat. He flamboyantly snapped his finger and Avery left the locker room.

Dre could not believe what he had seen. He snapped. Avery disappeared. *Who the fuck is this guy, Houdini?* Dre thought. With the locker room to them, Dre spoke calmly. "I don't know why you have been threatening me, but this shit right here, better be kosher."

"Listen, Dre, I have a proposal for you to make some good money—"

"I'm not interested in being your body guard."

"Funny," BG said. "I need you to use your influence and cop for me in Philly."

Dre's face turned angry. "You mean my blackness. What the fuck I look like letting you set me up? Fuck my chance up to go to USC, because I was caught up in some dope bullshit. Picture dat!"

"Set up! I'm talking about $800 a run to get down with me. Hell you're talking all this Lakers and Hollywood shit. Your people got cash, but not Beverly Hills cash."

What, dis mutha-fucka got my people bank account statements? "Come on. Why is it all of a sudden you need me? I've been in this school for two years and you've been doing your thing without me. You don't need me."

"Look, I'm not explaining myself, but, bottom line, Trigger got booked crossing the Mexican border with 1,000 bricks of fish scale in his trunk. I can't, as you know, take my ass back down North."

"I helped your silly ass once and you swear that I set you up. So why ask me again?" Dre shook his head and said, "This shit seem funny."

"Ain't shit funny. Trigger claimed that some dude named Ice probably had them young nigga's rob me. He wired my money. My bad for accusing you."

"First off, cracker," Dre said and pointed his index finger hard into BG's chest. "White boys cannot say nigga. Fuck what you see on TV and hear in raps." Dre let that sink in and then said, "I'mma help you out." He had sold his soul to the devil. "I'll cop for you, but I want $1,000 a run along with a rental car for each run. And you better not tell anyone this shit," Dre said sternly.

Without any hesitation, BG jumped on it. "No problem. Here's my new cell number." BG pulled a piece of paper from his pocket and handed it to Dre. "Meet me in the Sears parking lot at the mall tonight at nine o' clock."

"No doubt. Be there, *alone*." Dre warned.

* * *

Outside the locker room, BG pulled out his cell phone and dialed it. When the call was answered he said, "You were right. Enlisting a monkey was easy." He then added, "And it's true, all of them want to make a quick buck."

"And prisons prove they'll do anything to get it," the man on the other end remarked and then chuckled. The man ended the call, and then pressed stop on his recorder.

CHAPTER 4

Kareem waited in the long bank line for twenty minutes, aggravated, but patient. The moment when he approached a teller seemed like an eternity had passed. He smiled at her and thought, Act I, Scene 2.

He explained to her, he was a bank customer and headed to the University of Miami that summer. He looked at her coyly, and then added, "You're way too busy to hear my life story—"

"Please, go ahead. I could use the break."

"Oh! Since we're being honest, my dad sent me in here to handle this cash advance all on my own." He lied. "He bet my mother that I will get this transaction all wrong." He paused and glanced at the limo. The teller's eyes followed his. "Yeah, they are out there making wagers, right now, on whether I'll leave this bank with the cash."

The teller grinned. She was hooked onto his con. To fully reel her in, he passed her an Internet printout from the *Miami Herald*.

"I'm going to be staying here," Kareem told her, as her eyes widened at the monthly rent.

She read the ad aloud. "Coral Gables, two bedrooms—"

"One for my gear." Kareem interrupted her from deeply analyzing the ad.

"It must be nice. To do a cash advance, I'll need a credit card and ID."

Kareem slid the John Carter American Express and his counterfeit school ID across the counter. "I need two months rent, and two months security."

She looked over his credentials, but a $9,600 cash transaction needed more reassurance. "Do you have a license?"

Kareem leaned into the counter and whispered, "I hate to sound condescending, but Philippe drives. I simply ride."

The woman smiled, and three minutes later, Kareem walked out the bank $9,600 richer.

CHAPTER 5

*D*re stepped out the locker room and contemplated the problems that he faced dealing with BG. His pre-suburban days had been filled with hustling cocaine and weed on one of the meanest turfs in Philadelphia. He was arrested at William Penn High School and, Delores' wrath was lethal. His mother was especially upset to learn that he had skipped school and commited robberies and home invasions, even if they were against drug dealers. She was concerned for him sure, but she was more concerned with the misery that she'd face losing a son.

Dre walked into the school lobby and was greeted by a soft, passionate kiss from Tasha, his prize. Tasha had a jasmine hue and doe-like jade-colored eyes. She was beautiful and brainy, and tripled as the head cheerleader, and a member of the Math Counts team.

"So—do you miss your girl?" she whispered.

Dre loosened his grip on her and asked, "What kind of question is that? Of course, I did, Tash."

Tasha bent to pick up her books, but Dre grabbed her arm and told her, "I'll take these, cutie." Dre snaked his arm along her waist and pulled Tasha closer to him as they walked to her car. Her long, jet-black hair rested softly on her shoulders and blended perfectly with her black calfskin winter coat. Arriving at her dated Nissan Maxima, Dre thought about the new car that he would buy her.

His mind had played tricks on him. He had come too far to go back to his destructive behavior. College scouts across America wanted him for his football talent. A few schools had dual scholarships for his track and field performance, as well. He had hours to weigh his options. Prayerfully, the reasons not to hustle tipped the scale.

Dre tossed the bags into the back seat and entered the car. Tasha turned on the radio and tuned to Power99, the urban/contemporary station. She left the school grounds, as Usher's duet with Alicia Keys, My Boo, filled the car. Dre listened as Tasha sang and drove, affectionately looking over at him., He envisioned the first time that they had had sex. Tasha had moved as freely as she did when she caught pom-poms. Her gymnast flexibility added to her allure. The Nissan crossed route-202, and the song became an afterthought. Something new had consumed Dre and Tasha, as they watched Kareem walk out of a bank and get into the limo that Dre had watched pull off from the school moments earlier.

CHAPTER 6

*W*ith *$9,600 stuffed into his socks, Kareem emerged into the Four Seasons Hotel* and approached the front desk clerk. He had made a reservation en route to the fabulous hotel. He gave the clerk John Carter's credit card. She imprinted it and handed it back. She tapped a few keys on her computer, grabbed a receipt from the printer and had Kareem sign it. He did, *John Carter*, and she gave him a plastic key programmed to open his suite.

"I am a tad short on cash, could I have a cash advance?" Kareem asked, as he slid the American Express across the counter again.

Kareem walked across the lobby, $500 wealthier, and smiled to himself. The rush was palatable. He checked his watch and it read: 3:45. He needed to get home before the five o'clock activities school bus did, to avoid anyone from knowing that he was not at debate team practice, but fraud practice.

Before the lobby doors opened, and he was scott-free, the clerk called out, "Mr. Carter!"

There went the essence of his glory. *What could she want?*

Kareem became deaf, and continued to walk. A bellhop stopped him and said something, while pointing toward the front desk. Damn, he thought, as he walked back to the front desk.

"Mr. Carter. I inadvertently neglected to ask for ID. Could you let me copy your photo for our records?"

Oh, he thought. That's it. "My wallet is inside the limo, tucked inside of my luggage. As soon as I unpack, I'll bring it down to you." *Surely, you are not copying my face.*

Twenty minutes later, the Jaguar limousine parked on Philadelphia's trendy Walnut Street. Kareem stepped out the limo and rushed into the Ralph Lauren Polo boutique.

Within minutes, Kareem walked three long-haired cashmere sweaters, two track suits, and a large duffle bag to the counter. There was no line. He gave the clerk John Carter's credit card and moment later the register spat up a receipt.

Philippe opened the limo door for Kareem, as he exited the Polo shop. Kareem told the driver that he was headed to Banana Republic, to serve, conquer and destroy the establishment.

In Banana Republic, he found a chocolate, wool army coat and dark-navy wool flat-front pants. The pieces totaled $262. He handed the clerk the hot wax.

"Do you have ID sir?"

"No. I don't need it."

"Sure you do. BR policy states that any purchase over $250 must be secured by showing ID."

"Sir, I am unconcerned about any store policy of that sort. The law states that I do not have to show you any identification to make a credit card purchase. If you'd like, I'll have my lawyer tell the store manager."

"That won't be necessary," the man said and completed the purchase.

Kareem exited the store, but before he entered the limo, he discarded the receipt from both Polo and Banana Republic.

That a boy, Kareem. Never leave a paper trail.

Before heading back to the suburbs, Kareem toured the up-to-the-minute Walnut Street. Mr. John Carter bought him everything that he wanted from Burberry, Coach, Diesel, Distante, Puma, and Wayne Edwards.

CHAPTER 7

The polished rosewood table in the Bezel dining room was quiet, save for dinner forks meeting fine china. The Venetian hand-blown vase in the center of the table was home to fresh roses, the scent that filled the room.

Kareem Bezel, a lover of Italian cuisine, basked in his mother's savory lasagna. He looked around the table at everyone searching for the words to open the floor to a conversation. He found none. Surely, he could not speak about how he ravaged John Carter's plastic that day.

Eli, the step father, sat in his medical coat, eating and reading a medical journal. He was a biomedical engineer and he worked to stay on top of his profession, finding a cure for diabetes. Time had proven that Eli was a good man, especially since he believed that his wife did not have to work. He was not the poster boy for a caveman, though. Delores did run a home based interior decorating company.

Andre Bezel sat at the table without an appetite. So many things ran through his mind. Each thought passed the baton to another, in what seemed like a race to another galaxy. He looked around the table sure that he would destroy that happy home if he was arrested for selling drugs.

Dawn Berryman, Eli's only child by Delores sat in her chair with a glow on her face, so priceless that it could shelf Cinderella. Her two ponytails bounced vivacious curls each time she moved her head. She was an eight-year-old third grader that was more diva than student.

After dinner, Delores walked upstairs to Dre's bedroom door and heard, "I don't know what you heard about me, but I'm a mutha-fuckin' p-i-m-p." She gave the door a knock worthy of scaring a felon on the run, and then entered without his response. She lowered the stereo and Dre turned from staring out the window.

"Who the hell is that?" Delores asked him, disgusted by the vulgar line. Every since they moved to the suburbs she had a problem with hip-hop.

Dre chuckled and told her that it was 50-Cent.

"He raps more like he has no sense," she told him smiling. The suburbs had softened her up a tad. "Close the door when you're listening to that crap."

"Aiight."

"Why are you staring out of that window like that? What's on your mind?"

"This Probability and Statistics test tomorrow," he told her and pulled the textbook from the windowsill.

"I don't know how you're studying with that rapper adding his two cents," she told him and walked out the door.

He yelled, "That's 50-Cent, mom."

With Delores gone, Dre continued to mentally calculate the probability that he would become a drug-lord, and the statistics that he would be a seventeen-year-old in prison for life.

* * *

Kareem was in his room checking his investments on-line. He also scrolled through CNN.com for the latest world news. After he caught up on the current events, he pulled out his duffle bag and began to hang the clothing he—well, John Carter—bought earlier. On a shelf in his walk-in closet, he put all the pieces into their proper place, including the cash.

CHAPTER 8

At six-fifteen *that evening, Kareem pulled into the King of Prussia mall parking lot* and gave his car, a pearl white Lexus ES300, to the Neiman Marcus' department store valet. He had worked for the elitist boutique for two years and had access to his grandmother's car for about the same length of time. He checked his Etro tie in the valet booth mirror, before he and Dre shook hands and parted ways.

Dre had passed several of his classmates as he went to meet Tasha. The mall was a hangout for the Upper Merion High students. He could not wait to show Tasha off through the mall. He turned into the food court and instantly saw Tasha standing there with a pretty smile on her face. She jogged over to him and they hugged tightly. Tasha's younger sister Sasha and her best friend Talibah walked over to them. Dre and Talibah stared at each other intently. It was a lustful intent, indeed.

"Hey, Dre," Talibah said softly, not letting her voice go to the sexual octave she desired it to reach. Her chocolate complexion could put Hershey out of business. That day she wore light pink lipstick, and a tight short hair do.

"What's good, Tah and Sasha?" Dre replied smoothly, letting Tasha go.

"So, where to now, because I know you have been through here showing off," he told them checking out Tasha from head-to-toe.

"I don't know about them," Tasha said, pointing at her pals, "but, I'm going where ever my man takes me."

"Don't get cute because you have a boyfriend," Sasha told her sister and rolled her eyes.

"Not boyfriend. Man friend! Something that you need, okay, boo-boop," Tasha replied laughing. She grabbed Dre's arm and said, "Tootles. Call your girl when you're ready, or find a man, whichever comes first."

* * *

*K*areem walked around Neiman's men department. He was bored, but enjoyed work, and all of the benefits that came with it, but his mind was not there that night. That changed when Toi entered the department. His night was suddenly bright. They hugged as if they clung to life with the embrace.

"I didn't think that you were playing the mall tonight with you on punishment and all that jazz."

"My mom is trippin', but she let me come here. I have to buy a gift for my grandparent's anniversary."

"Oh, so she's using you to buy the gift," he said, jokingly.

Toi had an un-tanned, golden complexion, all wrapped tightly around a stature mirroring a Nelly video vixen. She was half Filipino and Black. The exotic look was lethal, but she had a lot of African features available to the eye.

"Slavery that I am cool with," she said, and stepped closer to him. She wrapped her hands around him and gave him an amatory kiss. "How else would I have given you that?"

"You couldn't, and I needed that," he said. He was mesmerized by her allure. His cell phone rang and he answered it. Dre informed him that he would get a ride home from the mall with Tasha, so there was no need for Kareem to wait for him. Kareem hung up and told Toi that he had to get back to work.

* * *

Later that night, Dre arrived to the Sears parking lot and spotted BG leaning on his Camry. He paced towards the car, and wondered what his life had in store after that transaction. He didn't believe the hurdles that he had jumped to get away from the drug game. And there he was up to his old criminal behavior again. What would Kareem think about his decision to follow in their father's footsteps and possibly earn a life sentence, just like dear old dad? There was no need to contemplate the question at that point. He was there, and going for it. Period!

"Glad that you could make it," BG said, as Dre approached him.

"Save the small talk. Where's my gym bag? Good lookin' for grabbing it from the field," Dre replied. He was properly preparing the tapes for possible undercover recordings.

BG looked at him perplexed and Dre ran his thumb over his four fingers, indicating for BG to show him the money.

"Just what I like, a true business man."

Dre ignored BG's quest to garner respect, as the white boy opened his trunk. He grabbed a gym bag with the high school logo on it and slammed the trunk shut. He passed the bag to Dre, and said, "That's $13,000 cash. I need a half-K of powder—"

"What the fuck are you talking about, clown?" Dre said cutting him off. He threw the bag over his shoulder, and asked, "Car keys?"

BG passed along the keys to a Chevy Impala and informed Dre that he needed to be careful with the rental. Dre, without a response, turned and walked to a white Impala. He jumped into the driver's seat, after he tossed the bag into the trunk. He pulled off into the night and left BG to wonder if he had been scorched again by Andre Bezel.

CHAPTER 9

*K*areem *closed his register and took the money bag to the customer service area.* He then walked out to the parking lot toward his car. When he arrived to the car, he mouthed, "Damn!" as he looked around hopelessly for security or a witness. "I do not believe this bull shit," he said, ranting. He threw a jab into the air. How would he explain to his grandmother that her car stereo was gone? His lap top in the back seat also was gone. And her front passenger window was gone, too.

He paced, annoyed, on the passenger side of the car looking at the broken glass, while he chanted profanities. He was further enraged that he had left his lap top on the seat and that may have tempted the thieves. Good thing that he had all of his school material backed-up on a travel zip drive.

He gathered himself and pulled out his cell phone to call Dre. He had to tell his older brother about his stupidity. Dre did not answer, though. Rather than leave a message, Kareem hung up as mall security arrived on the scene.

The frail, slick haired rent-a-cop stepped out of a security pick-up, holding a flashlight. He pointed it at Kareem, and blinded him. Kareem put his forearm over his eyes before the guard asked him, "Is there a problem?"

Kareem stepped out of the light, and told him, "Right now that silly ass light is the problem!"

"Excuse me! I beg your pardon! Is this your car?" Kareem nodded and the guard asked, "Do you have the registration and license to prove that?"

"What!" Kareem was pissed off. "I am not driving, so I don't have to show you shit. My car was vandalized and robbed, yet, you're questioning me. You should be looking foe the little bastards that robbed me." He reached into his wallet and tossed the man his ID. He then reached into the glove compartment through the broken window, and passed the guard the registration. It was that moment that he was glad that his father had put the car in his name. First, because the feds would have taken it had they knew about it. Second, Kareem had to be prepared for a driving while black assault.

Bozo scrutinized Kareem's credentials and then sarcastically asked, "So, Mr. Bezel, would you like to file a report?

"That would be a negative, pretending Officer Saminowski. You've proven your competence. No, thank you."

Kareem's mind swirled with anger. His car was robbed. He was mocked by a security guard. *This had to be karma*, he thought. John Carter was being avenged. He sped off and drove fast through the mall parking lot. After a long five-minutes drive, he parked in the family home garage and walked straight to Dre's room to tell him the bullshit.

He tapped on Dre's door and walked in, figuring that he was asleep. Dre was not there. At first, he was confused, but then it dawned on him that, Tasha had driven Dre home. He must have been at her house, in her dimly lit bedroom, playing R. Kelly.

CHAPTER 10

Dre drove along the Schuylkill Expressway, and he blared Mase's Welcome Back album; very smooth, but gangster. The title track described his mind frame, perfectly. He remained focused on each of his actions to avoid an unwarranted police stop. He was aware that becoming a trafficker was just as bad as being the dealer or manufacturer. His dad had schooled him on the drug game, but he had also acquired knowledge observing his surroundings, even after his dad was arrested. He knew that if he was caught, he was off to federal prison.

He drove the speed limit and, so many things played devil's advocate in his mind. Before he knew it, he viewed the picturesque Philadelphia skyline. He approached the Girard Avenue exit, and stared at the historic Boathouse Row with all of its lights illuminating the freeway. He prayed that this was not the last time that he drove along the Schuylkill River. Without handcuffs, and stuffed in a bloody, stinking, Philadelphia PD patty wagon, anyway.

He arrived at the drug infested, government deprived 17th and J Street intersection with an advantage, something that BG lacked: he was from the hood. BG showing up on that stage was easily mistaken for a member of Mayor Street's "Safe Streets" team—a task force of the PPD to rid Philadelphia of its increasing drug epidemic and rising body count. Dre was just a hood nigga, whose father was as legendary as Biggie.

Dre parked the Impala and approached, drug king-pin, Ice, known for his flashy diamond collection. He saw Dre's slim figure enter into his no-fly zone and couldn't believe that it was Dre.

"Dre, what the hell are you doing here this time of night?" Ice asked. He seemed concerned. He had not seen Dre since his move to the suburbs. Delores had also previously cursed Ice the fuck out for encouraging her son to follow in his father's footsteps.

"Dawg, it's a long story. To cut to the chase, I need some raw."

Ice walked away and indicated for Dre to follow. They entered one of Ice's dope houses and walked pass a wino slumped in the corner with a bottle of Wild Irish Rose resting on his lap. There was also, a young buck who received a blow job in the corner from an ogress crack head in another corner. Dre was not fazed. He had seen far more obscene shit on missions with his father.

Ice stepped into the kitchen and asked, "Tell me you have not started using this shit, out there with those white boys?"

Dre looked at him crazily and barked, "Hell no! I'm trying to get some of that suburban money, because it's definitely out there."

"Oh, I see. Well, why would I let you take my white customers?"

Dre could not believe his ears. *Go ahead, Dre*, the devil told him, *remind that pussy that your father made him.* Dre opted for a less controversial reply, though. He was not strapped, a mistake that he would not let happen again. He was there for one reason only. "We both can eat. I'll cop weight from you, and those white folks can stop blowing up the spot. You know they get followed from here and turn tapes in a heart beat when the feds stop them."

"How much weight you talking?" Ice asked curiously, after hearing the magic word, *weight*.

"That depends on your numbers. I need raw."

"Look—how much money you talking?" Ice asked getting closer to the dead presidents.

"What you want for a square? From me?"

"Damn, a whole square, huh? I'm thinking you came down for somthin' minor."

Ice sat back and thought what type of numbers he would throw at Dre. He knew that Dope had schooled Dre on the "Art of Drug Dealing," so to play the seventeen-year-old was not an option. Especially with a buyer that Ice knew could move on to the next man, easily.

Dre broke the silence and Ice's concentration. "Give me a number so that I'll keep coming back."

"Just on the strength of your pop, I'm gonna give you a square for twenty."

"Well, look, lemme get a half square," Dre said, and took advantage of the numbers, quickly.

Ice pulled out his cell phone and made a call to his runner. He spoke in a code and had his runner fetch the half-kilo that Dre wanted. He then informed Dre what he wanted would arrive in fifteen minutes. The prompt service was dubbed "The Fed-Ex of Cocaine."

Dre told Ice, "Take this ride with me to the Broad and Diamond Streets McDonald to count this quap."

Five minutes later, Dre parked in the McDonald's parking lot and Ice offered a meal on him. Dre was disrespected. Ice went into the fast food joint while, Dre went into the trunk to grab the cash. He thought about how he came up off the deal. He had extra ounces of coke and extra cash, all for simple negotiation. He couldn't wait to treat the extra coke as a commodity to inflate the coke price if a drought stumbled into the city. He was in a win-win scenario.

* * *

An hour later, Dre pulled back into King of Prussia and parked in a Genaurdi's supermarket parking lot off Route 202. He went into the trunk and separated his product from BG's without a scale. He thoroughly guesstimated, learning early in life how to weigh the product by eye.

Dre had a plan, and soon he would be on top. Screw a bank loan to start his accounting firm. He planned to stack his cash, buy into a firm and then get out the game. He didn't plan to fall victim to the drug game. He had learned from history. And he wasn't about to repeat it. Not knowingly, anyway.

How could BG think that I would be so naïve to let a white pussy pull one over on me? His slickest move was no match for my slowest, Dre thought as he walked to the Wachovia Bank adjacent to the supermarket and called BG. He told him to meet him in the supermarket parking lot. Dre waited and did his own surveillance for cops, and wondered what his brother did hopping into a limo in the same bank parking lot, earlier that day.

Minutes later, Dre watched BG approach the rental, as he looked around puzzled for his mule and drugs. Dre watched BG spin in circles, and felt his cell phone vibrating and knew it was BG. He ignored his calls.

Dre walked to the payphone in the shopping plaza parking lot and called BG from a public pay phone. He did not want any phone records linking him to late night calls with BG. When BG picked up, a disguised voice said, "The doors are unlocked, the keys under the visor, and the gym bag in the trunk." Nothing else needed to be said, and Dre hung up.

CHAPTER 11

*T*he next night, Kareem's much needed lunch break could not have arrived sooner. He walked to the employees lounge, punched out, and then walked through the lower level of the mall until he reached the corridor that led to the public bus depot.

He walked down the corridor until he reached a door labeled: MALL SECURITY. He knocked on the door and awaited a response. He stood against the wall and watched mall patrons pass him. He wondered if any of them were shoplifters. Mall security was strategically placed in the bus depot hallway to catch thieves trying to make it to a SEPTA bus. The buses offered a convenient vehicle from the city to the upscale mall.

The office door opened, and Kareem was signaled in by his friend, Joel. Joel had graduated from Upper Merion the previous year and was a member of Kareem's record-setting 4x100 relay team at the previous year Penn Relays. Joel made the video screening available without question. There had been a string of car thefts and purse snatchings in the mall parking lot, and Joel welcomed Kareem's assistance to nab the knaves.

Kareem sat in a small room filled with seven-inch television monitors. Each camera recorded the activity in any area of the mall and all points outside. After a twenty minute search, Kareem watched as Joel worked his walkie-talkie to assist two patrol cars with finding a thief who hid between cars to avoid capture. Kareem was amazed at the episode and had a heightened desire for the perpetrator to escape. Kareem, too, was a criminal and felt the man's pain.

Kareem turned back to the video. He watched and had become ill. He took his finger off the fast forward button, pressed rewind, and could not believe what he saw. His eyes widened and his eyebrows rose in disbelief. Jaws dropped at the unnerving sight.

He turned to be sure Joel was occupied before he slid the tape into his shirt. He secured it and buttoned his blazer to conceal the bulge. He walked over to Joel to say that he was leaving, but Joel waved him off, occupied, looking for the thief.

"I'll let myself out."

"The door code is 9-8-4-4-1," Joel responded, sure that he could trust the seasoned thief that he let into mall security headquarters.

* * *

*B*y nine that night, the night air was glacial as Kareem walked to his car after work. His mind raced with the analytic flair of a lifer on a shrink's couch making a case for parole. The contents of the tape had him vexed. He started the car and drove off, mapping how best to approach the situation.

Knowing Dre all his life did not make approaching him any easier, especially when the proposed conversational topic involved Dre's personal affairs. Kareem was well aware of Dre's desire for privacy, having watched him fight for it their entire lives with their mother. Family meant everything to Kareem, a force that propelled him to move back with his father's mother, Jean-Mary. No matter how he felt, Dre would be confronted when he got home, and not a minute later.

When Kareem walked into the kitchen and observed the red IN-USE light lit on the base of the cordless, he knew that it was Dre on the phone. Perfect because he had a lot to talk about.

Without a knock, Kareem barged into Dre's room and said, "I need to holla at you in a minute." He was stern and slammed the door as he left for dramatic chide.

Kareem went into his room and changed out of a fine Gucci suit and into Versace pajamas, both appropriately stolen. He brushed his teeth, and the returned to Dre.

Surprisingly, Dre was off the phone. Kareem sat in the desk chair and swiveled until his back was to Dre.

"Dawg, I do not know what's got you barging in my hut, but this better be worth me hanging up with Tasha," he said to Kareem's back.

"Oh, it's urgent," Kareem assured him, then spun around in the chair, clasping each arm of the chair with his hands using strangling force. "Look, I've been hearing some stupid shit about you selling drugs."

"Do not come in here on any he-said, she-said bullshit, because a nigga ain't tryinna hear that shit."

"At any rate," Kareem said to him. "What's this I hear you're out hustling with BG. Or is it for him?"

"What!" *How dis nigga know that?* Dre thought.

"You lied to me about Tasha taking you home last night, so that you could—"

"Mind my fucking business," Dre said, cutting him off. "Who da fuck you think you talkin' too?"

"You!"

"Nigga, you got me fucked up. Who the fuck got they eye on me, running and telling you like you my fuckin' dad? Tell those bitches you fuckin' to mind they fucking business, for a pop one of them hoes," Dre said and pulled out a Desert Eagle.

"You carry guns now, and have that shit in the house. You got the game fucked up. This person does not lie. So, Tasha drove you home last night?" Kareem couldn't believe it.

"Get out my room, nigga."

"You're a dumb-ass-clown. If Tasha was asked by the cops, would she confirm that she drove you home? Better yet, would Talibah and Sasha, considering they all left the mall together, and without you?"

Dre was numb, but he snapped, "Mind your fucking business, Kareem. Real rap! I'm a grown ass man. When I saw you hopping in that limo, did I run back questioning you? No! So, how 'bout you fall back, homey?"

Kareem thought that his hearing had failed to convey Dre's last statement. Suppose Delores had seen him? "You're right. My whole approach was wrong." Kareem confessed balming the atmosphere. "Lemme just say this: mall security records all activity."

"So does banks!"

Get the fuck outta here. "And mom or dad won't like you getting locked up, again," Kareem said, ignoring that reality.

"Investigated, not arrested."

"Same thing."

"And fuck your dad. Had he been out of jail, being a real father, maybe, I wouldn't be involved in this shit…"

"Hold the fuck up." Kareem growled and stepped into Dre's face. "Don't blame my father for your fucking stupidity. You should be learning from his mistakes, dumb-ass-nigga!"

"You're right. Your dad."

"Nobody put a fucking revolver to your dome and forced you to do shit."

"Nobody is the same person that moved you with grand mom Jean-Mary, and left her a Lexus, that somehow landed in your hands. You're his favorite son."

"You sound like a real bitch. You're the one who was bought off by Eli. Your step-dad. You liked his fresh kicks, and new gear. His money had you cooped up in Andorra, and now out here. You didn't want to struggle in the hood, just hang there. I begged to get away from that lame. You stayed and had it good, and your still a fuck up. And here's my stupid ass right here on your team. Fuck you, nigga!"

"You swear you're a genius. Get the fuck outta my room, before I shut your lights off.

Kareem cocked his head to the side, and raised his eyebrow. "Pussy, you can't beat me."

* * *

Kareem lay in his bed, not the least bit concerned about the fight that he had with Dre. He couldn't believe that Dre underestimated his smooth aura as cowardly. Dre, equally, could not believe the over-hand-right that landed over his eye, very unexpectedly. It was shameful that Dre had to have his lesson of the night beat into him: never do a drug deal in a mall parking lot.

CHAPTER 12

That hat weekend, Kareem awoke to the smell of breakfast, and rolled over, before he checked the alarm clock. It was nine-thirty a.m. The sun beamed through his window, but he was not convinced that it was warm outside.

He freshened up, stumbled into the kitchen, and found his mother cooking his favorite breakfast—bacon and cheese omelets, waffles, and fresh squeezed orange juice. This was the one thing that Saturday mornings brought to his home. Since they moved to the suburbs, he was forced to embrace a culture that he developed long before he moved there. It was easy when Jean-Mary drove him to Upper Merion, and he lived in the Germantown section of Philadelphia with her. Yet, over the past three months, he had successfully completed the crossover.

Delores did as well. She was in a local book club, and president of the Home and School Association. She was also the best interior decorator in King of Prussia. She used her urban spice to add flavor to the traditional suburban styles.

"Take that doo-rag off at *my* table," Delores said in her soprano tone. Everything that she said was in the possessive—"*my* study," "*my* lawn," and "*my* garage."

"Good morning to you too, mom," Kareem replied. He then informed her, "This is a wave cap, Mother, and perfectly legal at the kitchen table for breakfast, according to Molly Foster, the etiquette instructor that you send us to."

"Then eat breakfast as Molly's. Take that doo-rag off at my table."

There was that my, again, Kareem thought. He replied by snatching the doo-rag off. He exposed a sea of waves, and then made a plate. After he wolfed down the food, and excused himself from the table, Dawn stumbled into the kitchen. He picked her up and spun her in the air.

"Put me down." She demanded. She hated being treated like a baby.

After he placed her onto the floor, she asked, "Can you take me to the movies today. Mommy is busy?"

"I'm not going there, but I am going to dinner with Toi. If you want to go there, I'll take you with me."

"What about the museum?" Delores asked.

"Yeah, take me to the museum, brother, please." Dawn exclaimed, hugging him to convince him to take her. Now she wanted to be a baby.

"Mom, see what you've done. I don't have money for all that." He told her lying. He actually felt bad taking his mother's money when he was sure that he had more than her. Surely, he had to pretend that he was just as broke as any other sixteen-year-old, not born with a silver spoon. He had thousands invested with Merrill Lynch and a handsome coffer at Wachovia Bank.

"You take her and I'll pay for both you and Toi."

"Deal! Let me get dressed and make a run. I'll be back for her."

"What time, Kareem?" Delores asked with a sassy hand on her hip.

"One," he yelled as he went up the steps, nearly bumping into, and not acknowledging Dre, who came down the stairs.

* * *

Dre walked into the kitchen and rinsed his hands before he fixed himself breakfast. He didn't greet his mother or sister.

"Have you lost your ever lasting mind?" Delores asked him. "You don't walk into my kitchen as if you pay the damn taxes, and I'm the hired help. It's disrespectful to enter a room and not speak to the occupants."

"Hello mother. Hey, Baby D," he responded, somberly.

"Don't roll off that side of the bed again." Delores warned.

"Dre want to go with me and Kareem to the museum today?"

Dre didn't care to be in the same house with Kareem, let alone at a museum. He sat at the table in a throwback Sixers warm-up suit and Nike Air Force Ones. He had planned on eating and getting out of King of Prussia soon thereafter.

"No, not this time. I have other plans."

"Like what?" Delores asked, with a furrowed eyebrow.

"Like visiting Aunt Renee." He said that freely, knowing that he was not allowed anywhere near 17th and Jefferson Streets. He was forbidden from that area because his mother blamed the neighborhood for manipulating her son into becoming a menace like his father. She did not want him down there under any circumstances, and Andre Bezel's hardhead knew that.

Even though she had a dental hygienist certificate, Aunt Renee could not do anything with it. She remained in the grip of her crack habit, relapsing every time she got treatment. So there she was in the hood, living on the dole.

"You're not going to no damn, Aunt Renee's. And you know why. I will not have this talk with you again, and not in front of Dawn."

"But, I want to see..."

"You know, you never cease to amaze me, Andre. After living up here in a clean, quiet environment you want to be around such filth."

"Aunt Renee is not filth."

"Don't play with me. There's nothing down there. Nothing! You do not see Kareem wanting to be anywhere near that place."

He had heard enough and stood to walk out the kitchen. He stopped, to leave his mother with a thought: "I am Andre Alexander Bezel. I am not Kareem Jamel Bezel. The sooner that you recognize that we are two different people, the sooner you'll realize I'm not going to be a nerd, or go to Harvard. I can't wait until he messes up and ruins your perfect little picture."

Delores walked over to him and put her index finger into his chest. Steam rose from her forehead. "Don't-you-e-va-dis-re-spect-me-a-gain!" she said, warning him. Each syllable ended with a jab to the chest. "For all of that mouth, you can keep your black-ass in the house all weekend. You're going to be just like your sorry ass father: a jail bird. You can go to jail after you graduate and get from under my roof. If I catch you in North Philly, and I will, I promise that your room will begin to feel like a cell. Now get out of my kitchen!"

"Now get out of my kitchen," Dawn said, mimicking her mother. She added to Dre's feeling that everyone hated him.

Delores flopped into a chair. She was on fire. Hard as she worked to navigate her children to successful careers, Dre was determined to be defiant. She would not allow it, though. She steered him right, and was not having him veer left.

Dre walked to his room and wondered why his life was so complicated. He hated being compared to Kareem, especially, now that he knew, Kareem was not all that perfect.

CHAPTER 13

*K*areem showered and shaved fuzz from his cheeks. His alarm clock read ten-fifteen, and he needed to go. He was an avid reader of *Philadelphia Magazine, Robb Report, Architectural Digest, Ebony, Black Enterprise*, and *GQ*. Those magazines guided him into manhood. They taught him how to treat himself, a woman, where to entertain a woman, how to dress to impress her, and how to live as if he were rich. Well, for his age, he was.

He dressed in a mocha-colored Jean-Paul Gautier suit, cream Yoon of Italy dress shirt, and an off-white and chocolate Burberry tie. He complimented the earth-toned look with a Louis Vuitton icon print belt, loafers and wallet. He had a matching Louis Vuitton man purse, but he'd never wear it.

At his computer, Kareem removed the regular ink cartridge from his laser printer and replaced it with MICR ink—magnetic ink that allowed store registers to read the numbers on the counterfeit checks that he was about to create. He opened the check program on his system and entered all the required information that would print on the fraudulent checks. He had used bank routing numbers stolen from checks that he purloined from Neiman's customers. He substituted the legit account numbers with fake ones, with the same amount of numbers as the real ones. He did that to avoid any *real* customers from having trouble with their account. The checks printed out on sheets that contained three perforated checks. On each sheet the account number of each check advanced three digits to prevent the made-up account numbers from being flagged by check authorizations companies. He threw thirty checks into his wallet, along with a state-issued identification card that he paid a Penn DOT employee $200 for. With all of his bona fides in place, Kareem Bezel transformed into, one David Kritz.

* * *

*D*re heard Delores yell for him to pick up the phone and he snatched his cordless from the cradle.

"What's up, Dre?" Talibah asked him in a seductive tone.

"Chillen, who dis?" he asked, cautiously, as if he had not known.

"You don't know my voice by now?"

"Come on, don't play games," he responded sharply. He had to be sure that Tasha and Talibah were not trying to set him up. He'd kill them bitches.

"Don't be so mean. It's Talibah," she said, defensively, and then added, "What's up, sexy?"

"Me, sexy? No, you're the sexy one." He lied. She was a cute six, and he had Tasha the ten. "Why are you calling me?"

"I saw that stare at the mall."

"What stare?"

"You want to fuck me, Dre."

"Bitch, you high! I am married to your best friend."

"You two are hardly married. Married my ass. Speaking of ass, when you gon' hit this one?"

"You're crazy." Dre shook his head at how dirty Talibah was. There was no way that he would fuck her. His thought was interrupted by the other line. He checked the caller ID and mouthed, "Damn!"

He clicked over, and Tasha said, "Come outside, Dre."

CHAPTER 14

Kareem gazed into the blankness of the sky, as he drove to the bank. There was not a cloud in sight. That day was an artists' rendering of a picture-perfect day.

The car radio played 860 AM, Philadelphia's business/finance talk station. He tuned in just in time to hear Attorney General Janet Reno inform citizens how identity thieves had savagely beaten the economy to the tune of 9.9 billion dollars. Reno went on, "Identity theft is so devastating in its effect because citizens failed to check their credit reports last year. This year, we are up to 500,000 reported cases of theft."

Before Ms. Reno relayed the tips to protect the listeners from identity theft, Kareem changed the station, as he spearheaded the need for the tips. Never carry your social security card in your wallet, or give the number to anyone, especially not via telephone. Only throw away shredded credit card invoices, bank statements, or cancelled checks into the trash. Credit cards and checks that had been lost or stolen should be reported to creditors and banks immediately. Check your credit report every ninety days. Blah, blah, blah.

Kareem was tired of those irrelevant tips. He had methods to thwart all of the jazz. Had he possessed a stolen credit card, he called the creditor, before the victim and placed a password on the account. He also told the creditor to note that, he recently divorced and his wife threatened to have his cards cancelled, so they should be on the look-out for a male pretending to be him to call. He had harlots that worked in various places that had access to sensitive information. Janet Reno would be amazed at what he traded his dick to women for.

For one reason or another, Kareem was pissed at Janet Reno and someone had to pay for her ignorance. He absolutely could not tolerate her bullshit.

He grabbed his cell phone from the passenger seat and had Nextel connect him to the Hermes boutique in Honolulu, Hawaii. He informed the representative that he was Christopher Murdoch and..."I simply adored the Hermes sneakers advertised in the January 2003 GQ rag."

"Ah, yes, they're nice, right?" the salesman asked. "They come in brown, tan, and black for $525 each."

"I'll take all three colors in a size eight. I want to give them to my father as a gift. He'd jog in them and tear them up in a month." Kareem chuckled at his embellishment. He loved to lie.

"Mr. Murdoch, that's fine, but the address that you're shipping to must be the address on the credit card, or we must ship the sneakers to you and you can then forward them to dad. Is that okay?"

"Absolutely!" Kareem then read Mr. Murdoch's home address—315 Murrow Drive, Madison, Wisconsin—and Visa credit card number to the sales representative. The man placed him on hold to process the card, and Kareem hoped that the profile and credit card number was good. He had received it from his cousin Rhonda. She worked at the Nextel store in King of Prussia Mall, and her work was always good, but he was always careful. She privileged Kareem to mobile users that were approved for five lines or had an American Express on file for automatic monthly bill payment.

Mr. Murdoch's $1,575 purchase was approved and shipped via Fed-Ex. Kareem thanked the salesman and hung up the phone. With that complete, he made a mental check that task number one was accomplished, as he pulled into the Cedar Crest Savings and Loan Bank parking lot.

CHAPTER 15

Getting into her car, Dre was relieved that Talibah was not in it, also. It wasn't a set-up, but rather something urgent. He guessed. Tasha stared at him as he sat next to her before hugging him tightly.

She emoted, "Thank you, Dre. I really need you."

Dre hugged her tight, and asked her what was wrong. She managed to tell him that she needed for him to drive.

"Whatever you want," he told her, and exited the car.

Tasha slid over to the passenger seat as Dre walked around the front of the car. He hopped into the driver's seat and pulled off. He wanted to know what the problem was. It was not him cheating, or any rumor of him doing so. He turned the corner of his block, and they rode in silence. Their minds raced with thoughts of what was about to happen.

Being the man, Dre broke the ice. "Tash, what's the problem?" His tone was calm and would have coaxed Jaws.

"It's actually our problem, Dre."

"Our problem. Wouldn't I know about our problems?" He asked curiously.

"Trust me. Its our problem," she told him directly.

"Okay, Tasha. What's our problem?" He asked becoming annoyed.

"We're pregnant!"

The tires screamed and could be heard for miles. He pulled over, dazed by the devastating blow. *We're pregnant? Who?* He thought. He choked and bluntly asked, "Who's the father?"

"Who's the father! Are you out of your fucking mind, Dre?" She screamed.

"Look! There's no way I can be the father. For one, you've cheated on me. More important, I'm seventeen with a partial academic and sports scholarship pending to USC, I can't be the father."

"We're not going into that cheating shit again. Period! You're the damn father. That cheating issue is dead and, he can't be the father."

"And why not?"

"Because, Dre, we used protection!" She had confessed it after denying having sex with someone else for so long.

"You used what! Bitch, you fucking told me that you didn't fuck him." Now all of a sudden she was pregnant. Dre was young, but very street wise. She would not pull any stunts on him. Dre put the car in drive, made a U-turn, and headed back toward his house.

"Where are you taking me?" she asked weeping.

"The fuck back to my crib."

"Dre, please," she screamed, pulling his arm. He swerved in the traffic. "This is our baby. You can't do this to me."

"Watch me."

29

"So, what are you going to just leave me?" she asked him, searching for love.

"Tasha! Even if the baby is mine, I can't do the baby thing. I have things to do in my immediate future."

"Andre, are you telling me to get an abortion, because, I'm not! I'll have this baby with or without you."

"Then do it without!" he said and slammed the car door shut, after he hopped out.

CHAPTER 16

"How can I help you today?" Jim asked. His soft voice contradicted his calloused features.

Kareem expressed his interest in an account that had no ATM usage fees, no minimum balance, and overdraft protection.

"We have the perfect account for your needs," the man said, but Kareem knew that. "The Express Checking account best suits your needs, mister, what did you say your name was?"

I didn't, but: "Its Kritz, David Kritz." Kareem responded.

"Mr. Kritz, this account is perfect because it allows you to write an unlimited number of checks per month, and unlimited free ATM usage. The downside to this account is that any in-bank transactions are subject to a $2.50 fee."

Kareem gave Jim his non-driver's ID and credit card advance check for $5,000. The credit card advance check was stolen from the mailbox of Jared O'Brien. Sorry Jared, you probably waited for these checks.

After entering all of the information into the system, Jim grabbed his telephone and called ChexSystems—a company banks conferred with to ensure that they did not open an account for someone who had misused an account at another bank. Naturally, David Kritz was given the green light.

Off the phone, Jim opened his drawer and pulled out a starter checkbook and a Welcome Packet, for his new customer. He also had a plastic Visa check card. Jim walked over to a printer and retrieved a sheet of paper that Kareem signed. Afterward, Jim went to the teller's area and made the initial deposit on the account. Back at his desk, Jim handed Kareem a yellow receipt and a $2,500 cash withdrawal.

Kareem walked out the bank and contemplated the other moves that he had for David Kritz's—well, his—account. He had nine other cash advance checks and by the time the fat lady sang—and, she would loudly—all of the checks would be deposited into the account and eventually withdrawn. He pulled from the parking lot, and tasted the $50,000 that he would get. He smiled at himself in the rearview mirror. His second job for the day was complete.

CHAPTER 17

*D*re stretched out on his bed, glass of cherry juice in his hand, the stereo remote on his nightstand within arm reach. He knew his plans for the future were at risk of derailment, but he was calm nonetheless. He somehow enjoyed the sense of relaxation, taking time to analyze the events surrounding him, both past and future.

Before moving to King of Prussia, he had had a good life and did not need the perfect-ness of residing in the suburbs. He had had an interesting and undoubtedly challenging transition.

His vision of chasing "90210" babes on Rodeo Drive, while he attended USC, had been unbearably clouded. All he could see was a flood of diapers being changed, soaring day care costs, and astronomical toddler education expenses. Dre was horrified at the thought of being a father so young. He practically forbade Tasha from using the word *baby* within 500 miles of him. Wasn't she on birth control? He wondered. Then asked: *Why I didn't take that matter in my own hands. I knew I should not have fucked her raw.*

He was confused, with no direction. Who the hell could he talk to? His mother would flip, if she knew about the breaking news developing under her roof.

The telephone rang, and he thought it was Tasha, as he swung his feet to the floor and sat up ready for war. He contemplated answering the phone on the second ring, because he could not lose his queen over this.

"Dre! Pick up the phone," Delores yelled up the stairs.

What am I going to say to this girl? What would I become if I became a father before my high school graduation? Why the fuck is this happening to me? "Hello." He spoke cautiously into the receiver.

"Dre?" His father was bemused at Dre's subtle tone. "Boy, why do you sound all down?"

How the hell did he pick that up? Am I that obvious? "I'm chill," he said and paused. "What's da deal, homey?"

"Same old jail shit, but what's good wit' chu? I can hear it all in your voice."

"I'm good."

"Boy, I've known you for seventeen-years. Is your mother trippin' on you or something?"

"Always, but it's not her."

"Oh, that chicken-head girlfriend of yours got you sprung, Dre?"

"She's a dime!"

"I don't give a fuck. Well, what's her baggage? All the dimes have some."

"She pregnant. With your grandchild, I guess."

"Oh, shit! Pregnant?"

"Tell the whole cell block," Dre said sarcastically. "Don't tell my mom, yo."

"Ok, but what you plan to do about that?"

"I don't agree with abortions, but she cheated on me, Dope. And I wanna move to LA."

"Yo, you are slippin' calling me my street name on these federal airwaves. You would regret an abortion. You gotta take this blessing, because what if later you can't have a kid. You have to get a job to get the bread to handle business."

"A job? You didn't work a fucking job! I'm going on the block. This some bullshit. Have you saw me with a ball? I am not trying to be like you and my mom all tied up at sixteen with no damn money."

"Hold the fuck up, dude. I don't regret having you or Kareem. Yes, it was hard, but I handled my business."

"Look where handling your business got you, D…, I mean dad. Just brilliant, right?" Dre asked, sardonically.

"That was a low joint right there, but it's cool, little nigga. I won't be in here forever, I hope you know that. I made mistakes, but I made them to take care of mine. Now you gotta take care of yours. This phone is about to hang up, so tell Kareem…"

Dope was cut off, once again. He would have to wait until the next time he called to finish that conversation. *Thanks, Dope. Thanks a lot. Thanks for nothing!*

Dre sat in bed and let his father's call linger momentarily and anger him more. To eliminate the stress, Dre smiled, grabbed his cell phone and made a call that would take his mind off his drama.

CHAPTER 18

*K*areem pulled into the shopping plaza adjacent to Willow Grove Park Mall. He was prepared to complete his third job of the day.

He casually strolled into a Ross department store, smiling at the young saleswoman at the register who nodded at him. Rather than grab a cart, Kareem walked to the home décor section. He grabbed a $199.99 bed-in-the-bag and a full size Aerobed worth $179.99.

He approached the counter, and was greeted by a gray haired woman with a look that screamed mid-life crisis. She said to him, "These things are nice. Are they gifts?"

Although that would be a fabulous excuse for the purchases, stick to the original script, the devil whispered to Kareem.

"No, I wish they were. They are for my college dorm."

"Oh! Congratulations. What university?"

Damn, she's in the business. Go ahead and really sell it to her.

"Princeton." He lied, smiling. "Could you ring these items up separately?"

"Sure, no problem. Cash, check, or charge?"

Oh, let's see, the devil joked into Kareem's ear.

"Check, ma'am," Kareem told her and paid for the bed and comforter set with two different checks. He had 28 checks to go.

Kareem placed the Ross purchase in the trunk of the Lexus, and then headed to Michael's an arts and crafts store. He proceeded to the faux flower arrangements and picked up a wicker basket arrangement worth $199.99. *That's perfect,* the devil said. *But look over there at the gold vase. That's $329.99. We need that in the trunk.* Kareem walked both pieces to the clerk and asked her to ring them separately.

She asked, "Why are you paying for these separately."

To which the devil wanted to reply, *none of your fucking business, bitch, just ring my homey the fuck up!* "I'm buying gifts for each of my grandmothers and I'd prefer to give them their own receipts, so that they can exchange them, if they choose too."

The cashier responded, "Oh, I see." She was not convinced by his lie.

"Look at the price difference. They both live in the same retirement development. Can you imagine the jealousy between the two of them? It would be obscene," Kareem told her smiling.

He pulled out his checkbook to pay and the clerk retrieved a three-ring binder. In the binder was a list of people prohibited from writing checks at Michael's, because a check previously written had bounced. David Kritz did not appear there, and he—David Kritz, that is—grabbed his two receipts from the clerk, and said, "Thank you. I'm sure they're going to love these."

Kareem checked the time and went on a bad check rampage. At Dick's Sporting Goods, Kareem bought cleats, a pair of Nike's and a tennis racquet. After writing two checks, the store manager encouraged him to write a third bad check for a $329.99 cow-hide racquet cover, and he did.

Kareem jumped behind the wheel of his car and cued E-Ness's *My Hood* single to blare through the stereo system. Quickly, he ran into Circuit and bought a VCR/DVD player, Playstation 2, along with two games. Finished that, Kareem headed to Genaurdi's supermarket. Not for food. For gift cards. He bought Nordstrom, Bed Bath & Beyond, Circuit City, Blockbuster Video, Shell Gas, and AMC Theater gift cards, all of them paid for with a bogus check.

It was after twelve-thirty, and Kareem needed to stop all the chitchat trying to convince store clerks of his legitimacy. He was utterly, David Kritz.

* * *

Before Kareem reached Toi's, he stopped at the storage company and dropped off his day's earnings. The purchases would remain there until they were due to be returned in ten days. He wished that he could thank the company heads for establishing the return policies. By his estimate, he would get back $6,500 in ten days for two hours, worth of work—more money for his stash. The separate checks assured him the cash refunds. Any refund over $300, in most cases, required him to receive a check in the mail, a check that wouldn't ever arrive. The two purchases ensured him a cash refund, because each individual transaction would fall below that "check by mail" threshold.

He pulled out the storage property, and smiled. He was elated about his day of making money, and couldn't wait to do it again.

CHAPTER 19

*T*he urbane South Street vibe cast a serene feeling over Dre, mellowing his mood. The street, comparable to New York's SoHo or LA's Melrose Avenue—well, not exactly—was chock full of small boutiques offering the latest trends in fashion and food to Philadelphia.

Joel Berberena—to those that knew him, Chino—drove down the strip slowly. They were gawked by envious pedestrians and jealous onlookers alike. Somewhere in that mix, Dre and Chino found a bevy of easy girls that desired to ride in Chino's Benz-745. The streets were good to Chino. He was fronted—weekly—a sizeable amount of cocaine to stay afloat, but not enough to lock down the area that he sold his product. Definitely, not enough to take over the game.

Chino parked on the corner of 5th and South just as a space became free. He stepped out the car, and reached in his Evisu jean pocket for change to feed the meter, because South Street beat cops would have the car towed for kicks. He donned a crisp white button-up and butter-colored Timberland boots. Despite the frigid weather, he only wore a soft leather Polo jacket.

Dre, along with other pedestrians, looked at the fly guy as if he was a rock star. The woman looked at the five-feet-seven-inches tall, half-black, half-Columbian, and his ponytail lustfully. Chino ignored the stares, assuming the women were beneath him.

The homeboys paced up the street to the smell of food floating from the various restaurants. They arrived at the Foot Locker and the sight of a pregnant girl in the back of the store buying infant Nikes had mesmerized Dre.

Chino tapped him, "Dawg, we ain't doing no stressing."

"Fall back, Chino," Dre told him.

From the time they were both students at Germantown High School, the two had bonded. Dre had a particular loyalty for Chino built on his stand up character. During a high school craps game in a G-Town High bathroom, Dre and Chino were both taken to the 14th police district for possession of cocaine on school property. Albeit, Dre sold drugs at the school occasionally, on that particular day the entire recovered product belonged to Chino, who bit the bullet and received an expulsion. Dre was suspended for gambling on school property. That was a major catalyst to Delores relocating to King of Prussia.

Dre gathered himself and unzipped his Woolrich coat. He scanned the athletic sneakers and selected gray Air Force Ones with a red Nike logo. The sneakers complimented a gray Polo sweat suit with a red Polo logo that Kareem had ripped someone off for to give to him.

After they purchased the sneakers, they walked down the animated strip to Dr. Denim, a premiere urban street-wear boutique. They both searched for something new and hot to sport to the club.

Dre approached, Alana, a saleslady, and told her that he was looking for some gear to separate him from the rest of the Philadelphia dudes. She told him that she could help him, and asked him about his budget.

"Budget! What the hell is that?" Dre said with a sly grin on his face.

Alana walked him over to the Roc-a-wear section and started pulling out pieces. Dre stopped her before she wasted her time. He told her that he wanted something new, but not regular.

With the sartorial, Kareem as his brother, Dre knew one-of-a-kind pieces when he saw them. Alana pulled out a pair of Evisu jeans. Dre looked at the price tag and masked his astonishment. He didn't see the point in paying for $300 jeans, but Chino was treating. To match the jeans, Alana pulled out an assortment of Indigo Red shirts and Dre chose one. The year 2002 had brought back trucker hats, and she tossed Dre a fresh out of the box, Ed Hardy one.

CHAPTER 20

*W*hen Kareem arrived to Toi's house, her mother, Diane, was in the driveway about to pull out in her car. He blocked her in, got out his car, walked over to her window and asked how she was doing?

"I couldn't be better."

"I promise to have her home by ten o' clock tonight."

"Kareem, that's not a problem. Just be careful with my baby."

"Always."

Kareem gave her a coy grin and headed to his car to back out the driveway, so that he could let her out. She pulled out and they both honked their horns at each other, before he pulled back into the driveway. Kareem parked and then went into the trunk to get a gift that he bought Toi. When he closed the trunk he saw Toi peering through the double storm door, alerted that he was there by the car horns.

Toi greeted him with a passionate kiss, ignoring the gift in his hand. He dropped the wrapped gift and groped Toi, pulling her closer to him. She pressed her pelvis against his, and she felt the bulge in his pants pressed against her. That was what she wanted. Toi was a virgin and Kareem didn't mind her keeping it that way until she was ready to give him that part of her. Kareem was being pleased in the bedroom elsewhere. Toi was more than a piece of ass to him. She was his future. His mind told him to pull away from her, but the scents from her Victoria's Secret body lotion and Escada perfume kept him near. When she was satisfied that she had teased him enough, she let him know that they needed to leave.

He followed her to her bedroom so that she could finish getting dressed. He lay across her bed and envisioned the day that they made love in it. He suddenly ran downstairs to get the gift that he had left behind. When he returned, Toi opened the gift and found a poster-sized picture of Kareem at the 2002 MTV Video Music Awards in New York City.

"You can pin me up to the wall with all of your celebrity boyfriends."

"Or I can post it to throw darts at you when I am mad at you!" she said and nudged his head.

* * *

*W*hen Kareem pulled onto the Benjamin Franklin Parkway, he disagreed with the low marks that *Conde Nast Traveler Magazine* had given Philadelphia for style and appearance, or the lack of them. Downtown Philadelphia was gentrifying. New shops and restaurants added color and life to the streets and drew trendier crowds from the Philadelphia suburbs. Conventioneers flowed in and out of the new hotels. And the city government had done its part: Mayor John Street had committed funds for landscaping, street improvements, promoting the city's new image, and the "Parkway"—the city's grand strip—glowed with the colorful flags of dozens of countries.

Kareem found parking on 20th Street in a lot labeled "For Museum Patrons Only." He grabbed their coats from the back seat and noticed that Toi was as stunning as a celebrity. She was dashing in a multi-color Versace silk blouse with a matching skirt, that fell below her knees. Fendi shades, Prada Donna purse, and Manolo Blahnik pumps further accentuated her beauty. She resembled a work by Picasso. Kareem worked at Neiman's and that paid off beautifully.

He grabbed her and they walked the half-city block to the Franklin Institute, Kareem having forgotten all about his younger sister. They entered the turnstile at the museum and were met by a giant Tyrannosaurus Rex. Kareem took their coats to the coat check and then they toured the wonderful world of the sciences.

* * *

The opening stretch of South Broad Street was "Baby Broadway," but the city had named it the "Avenue of the Arts." Along it laid the Kimmel Center for the Performing Arts, the Merriam Theater, the University of the Arts, and the Academy of Music. That day was the last showing of the season's "The Nutcracker" at the Academy of Music. Kareem hoped to get two tickets.

At the ticket booth, he asked, "Are there any seats available for the six o'clock showing?"

"Yes, they're $17 in the amphitheater."

"That's all?" Kareem knew that those seats needed binoculars. He could not have Toi up there.

"Well, we do have recently cancelled, fourth row in the front parquet, but they are $110 seats. I'm sure you're not interested in those."

Is this whore trying my pockets? "Let me get six!" He planned to donate the rest of the tickets to street persons, and then sue the theater, if they were denied admittance to the show.

* * *

After the show, at Twenty21, a hostess guided them to their reserved table. He left Kareem and Toi with two American continental cuisine menus. The menus had some of the most exquisite entrees on this side of the Pacific. The menu also contained an extensive assortment of expensive wines and spirits.

Kareem reviewed the menu while Toi was enthralled by the ambiance of the candle lit, cozy restaurant. She was further transfixed by the courtyard fountain view their table afforded them.

"This place is for the wealthy," Toi finally said.

"Well, tonight we are Vegas whalers, baby."

A flamboyant waiter, whose name tag read "Nay-Nay" approached their table, and asked, "How may I serve you tonight?"

Toi made the ordering process very difficult, asking how much things cost. Kareem and the waiter wanted to scream. If you had to ask the price, you had no business buying it.

"She'll have the shrimp scaloppini, and I'll have the Porterhouse, well done, with the Twenty21 sauce and potato fries."

"And your drinks?"

"Sure. Two daiquiris."

"Both virgins?" Nay-Nay asked. Everyone chuckled, as Nay-Nay butter-flied away to the waiter's area to input their orders.

"I can order my own food," Toi said when Nay-Nay was out of hearing range.

She's mad, so I guess she'll be throwing darts tonight, Kareem thought. "Listen," he began angrily, before she cut him off.

"I am not mad at you, Kareem. I actually liked that you ordered for me."

Kareem smiled as his cell phone rang, and interrupted his reply. He looked at the caller ID and excused himself from the table, relishing how he had the eighteen-year-old Latoya Eala eating out of the palms of his tiny hands, that were made for forgery, not labor of any kind.

When he reached the bathroom door, he flipped his cell phone open and heard, "Yes...Telecheck...My name is Donald Graham and my personal check has just declined...Oh, the check amount is $3,849.22...The numbers at the bottom of the check are as follows, the bank routing number is 021549864, account number 65454, and the check number is 8459...My state ID is issued from Pennsylvania and the ID number is 75254698—"

"Put the idiot on the phone," Kareem told his best friend and partner in crime, Marquis.

Marquis replied, "You want someone from the store...Hold a sec."

The clerk said hello into the receiver, and Kareem transformed into a Telecheck representative. "Madam, can I have your store merchant number?"

"Uh, yes, it's 987565254," the store clerk replied, following the normal procedure and giving Kareem the vital information.

"Would you read me the numbers at the bottom of the customers check from left to right?" After she read the numbers that Marquis had just rattled off, Kareem asked if the address on the check matched the address on the ID. She confirmed that they did, and he told her, "That was a code-1 decline. We just needed more information for the large amount of the check. Your approval number is 9745."

By the time Kareem sat back at the table, his cell phone rang again. He answered it and Marquis had told him that he had bought a sixty-inch plasma TV with HD. Kareem asked why the TV was so cheap. Marquis had put the balance on a stolen credit card. What mind boggled Kareem, albeit it wasn't a problem, was that store registers accepted any numbers as the approval-code. The numbers were not linked to the company giving the authorization. What a shame?

"Listen, I'm at Twenty21 with Toi. She said hi, but I'll holla at you later."

"Twenty21 and she's still a virgin," Marquis said, and then added, "You're whipped."

* * *

During their ride home, Toi and Kareem reviewed their dreams, goals and aspirations. They often brainstormed what their future together had in store. Pure puppy love. He wanted to be a designer and she wanted to be a fashion writer. "We'll be like Tom Ford dating Anna Wintour," Toi said confidently, comparing them to the head designer for Gucci and the *American Vogue* editor, as she hopped out the car and jogged into her home.

Kareem backed out Toi's driveway and had his Nextel operator connect him to Hermés in Hawaii. When the Hermés salesman replied, he told the rep that he wanted the tracking number of his package, which she gave him. He then called Fed-Ex. Posing as a Hermes salesman, he changed the shipping address of his three pair of sneakers to 1652 Martin Luther King Boulevard, apartment 6, Bronx, New York 12158. Marquis was a theater major at New York University, and he would pick the package up from the Mailbox Etc. store when it arrived the next day.

First place, Kareem Bezel!

CHAPTER 21

*L*ater that night, Chino pulled in front of Chrome Nightclub on Delaware Avenue. The atmosphere was festive. The chilly night air did not serve as a deterrent for the scantily dressed bevy of honeys outside the club. Dre rolled down the window and sniffed the fresh scent of the Delaware River that served as a back drop for the night club.

The two of them stepped out the 745 and Dre saw how all eyes seemed to be on them. That was cool for Dre, who needed the attention of a effervescent woman to flirt with and waste money on a cheap motel to fuck that night. Chino didn't care that Beanie Segal was performing; all he looked forward too was some new pussy.

At the VIP entrance, Dre tried to pick up the admission tab, but Chino stopped him because he was entering for free. The doorman slipped them both armbands that proved they were old enough to drink and they bounced into the club. They walked toward the steps that led to the second floor, and Antonio's hand was snatched up by a bodacious, florid-faced woman, who dragged him to the dance floor when the reached the top of the stairs.

Sean Paul's *Get Busy* blasted through the speakers as Chino and Dre parted ways to do their own thing. Dre was only seventeen, but he had been stealing sips of Courvoisier each time he went to Jean-Mary's. He leaned on the bar and ordered a double shot of the cognac. He sipped it and welcomed the scorch in his throat.

With Chino on the dance floor, Dre suavely bobbed his head to Beyonce's *Naughty Girl*. He listened intently to the words, as Tasha and the baby swam back to the surface of his thoughts. He needed a naughty girl to take his mind off Tasha.

He took another sip of his drink and a set of perfectly tanned breasts had his attention. The caramel hued bombshell sat next to him, enveloped in a leather halter top and leather blazer, which laid carelessly off her slender shoulders. He wanted a nipple to pop out. Her black Apple Bottom jeans rested perfectly over her spiky boots. Each time that the strobe light hit her, Dre admired her. She admired him the same, according to her sneaky glances.

Her dark eyes searched him as if she could see through his clothing. He told her, "All you have to do is ask to see, ma."

She smiled.

Dre swallowed the last of his drink, ignoring the scorch in his throat. He turned to the bartender and told her, "Let me have some Dom P."

"A glass of Dom Perignon coming up," the bartender said.

"No! The bottle," Dre said, correcting her, showing off for the bombshell.

The barmaid sat the chilled bottle on the bar and Dre paid the $275 bill. He cracked the bottle and poured himself some of the champagne. Dre bobbed his head coolly to the LL Cool J track *Head Sprung*.

"You're not going to drink that alone, are you?" The bombshell asked. He knew that she would.

He looked into her eyes and became mesmerized by her allure. He could not find the words to say to her, so he asked the barmaid for a glass and poured her some.

"Thank you," the woman said. "Sexy and polite. I'm Lisa."

Dre took her hand and told her his name. Her hand was soft and Dre envisioned touching other parts of her silky body. She was a little on the mature side, and Dre knew that she was a part of the Chrome college crowd. He was barely out of high school, and had an old head on his top.

He asked her, "What's a college girl like you doing in this hood joint?"

"I'm out of college. Twenty-five, babe."

Damn, I knew she was on old head, but she a quarter, Dre thought.

The two of them became acquainted, smiling and occasionally giggling at each other's lame quip. Dre was lost in her world and out of his world of teenage pregnancy and drug dealing.

At least for then.

* * *

Sulking in another area of the club, Tasha heard Talibah say: "Girl, Dre is over there without a care in the world with some bitch that has enough weave in her hair to be used by five bitches."

"You're lying!"

"Child, no, I'm not," Talibah said pointing.

"That nigga has a lot of fucking nerve. But I can't trip, yet. Let's move to get a closer look," Tasha responded, calmly.

"Fuck dat! Let's go kick the bitch's ass. And his!"

"No, I'm here, so he may be chatting innocently."

"You're here, yes, to see Beans. You don't have these broke ass nigga's all up in your face."

"Tab, chill. Let's move closer and if things get out of control, we gon' set it off up in this bitch!"

Tasha and Talibah walked over to the bar. Tasha eyed Dre like a hawk. Even though her nerves were plucked, she had never let her friends see her sweat. She would handle this without anyone else in her ear. Maybe that was the wrong approach, but she didn't give a fuck.

* * *

"So, Dre, do you have a girlfriend?" Lisa asked.

"Naw, I'm still getting over a break-up."

"Oh! That's crazy. How could a girl mess up with a fine brother like you?"

"I'm not as fine as you, beautiful."

Dre was so wrapped in his conversation with Lisa that, he hadn't noticed that Beanie Segal had performed and left the stage.

"Well, Dre, the club will be closing in fifteen minutes. I guess we can exchange numbers."

"Yeah, we can do that."

Tasha looked on as Dre's acquaintance dug into her purse. Tasha expected the bitch to pull out a pen, and she did. Tasha bumped and pushed her way over toward her man before he made the mistake and got slapped in front of the entire club.

Lisa jotted her number on a napkin and held it out to Dre. Tasha intercepted the number, balled it up and dropped it into Lisa's champagne glass.

"He won't need that," Tasha said, staring hard at the both of them. She then continued: "Dre, what the fuck you doing with this bitch all up in your face?"

"Bitch? Who the fuck you calling a bitch, little girl?" Lisa asked.

Dre smoothly interjected before things got out of control. "Lisa, this is my girlfriend, Tasha, I just told you about." He turned to Tasha, and said, "I was just telling her about us before you came over here drawin'. What are you doing here?"

"Do not fucking question me, Dre! Why was this bitch, as I said, all up in your face, nigga."

"Tasha, you are trippin'. We were talking as you saw. What, I can't talk to women in a crowded ass club?"

"You sound like a drunk."

"Dre, it was to nice meet you. I'm out of here."

"Bitch, bye!" Tasha told her.

Lisa ignored her and walked away.

"You're acting like a real stupid…"

"Like a what, Dre? A bitch?"

"Look! I'm out of here. That's why I don't want to have a baby by you now," Dre said, grabbing the last of his champagne and drowning it.

"You weren't ready to leave when that entire weave was all in your face. You're not giggling now."

Chino walked over to the quarreling couple and told Dre he was ready to go.

"You can leave. He's coming with me," Tasha told Chino.

"Actually, ma, I already have some pussy lined for him," Chino replied. "You'll have to get his number and get in line, because if he doesn't fuck this chick, then I do not get to fuck her girlfriend."

"Well, I'm his wife, and he's taking me home. So, you won't be getting that pussy tonight!"

CHAPTER 22

The Bezel's home telephone rang at the hour that an emergency had to be afoot. The call startled the entire household. Kareem and Delores said hello into the phone simultaneously.

The voice on the other end was Marquis'. It was 1:47 a.m.

Delores politely told him, "Marquis, Kareem has a cell phone. You can call him on that this time of the night. But I'd prefer if you didn't disturb him this time of the night, either, but that's his prerogative."

"Sorry, Ms. Delores."

They all hung up. Kareem didn't utter a word. He called Marquis' cell phone and when he answered, he barked, "Are you out of your mind?" He was so bossy, and that irritated Marquis, but hey, who cared. "Why the fuck would you call my house phone this damn late."

"Chill. I hit the wrong speed dial. Meet me at the 40-40 Club."

"Mar-Mar, you gotta be kidding me. It's two in the fucking morning."

"Listen, it's an after-after party, over at noon, and Jay-Z has plenty of rich bitches at his club trying to fuck."

"By the time I get dressed, drive to Amtrak, get the 4 a.m. train, it'll be six by the time I get a hotel room."

"Perfect timing. The other clubs will be closing and the bitches will flood the 40-40."

This fool says perfect timing.

Kareem got up and grabbed a quick shower using the half bathroom in the basement to avoid having to lie to his mother. He slipped on a Burberry denim suit and a Dolce & Gabbana denim tuxedo shirt. He grabbed his "H" icon printed Hermes coat and slipped on Versace military boots. He would lace them at 30th Street.

* * *

*D*re exited off the E-way in King of Prussia, relieved that Tasha and Talibah did not talk shit the entire ride back. His mind swirled with thoughts of Tasha's and his future. *Is this the beginning of the end?* He turned into his neighborhood and passed through his street en route to Tasha's mom crib. He rode pass his house, and Tasha had her head rested on his shoulder. Suddenly, he jerked and she moved, not understanding what made him shake. He leaned up to be sure that he looked at his brother's Lexus pull out the driveway, and turned toward the Schuylkill Expressway.

Where could he be going? Dre looked at the car clock *and* this late. He vowed to stay out of Kareem's business just as he expected Kareem to stay out of his. With that in mind he continued to drive as if the incident had not occurred.

* * *

Two hours later, in a taxi, Kareem instructed the driver to take him to Fifth Avenue and 59th Street. The driver deposited him in front of the world-renowned Plaza Hotel. If the kid in Home Alone Lost in New York could get over on the hotel, he could. This had been Kareem's millionth-time checking into the hotel under a different name. He was amazed that the front desk clerks remembered his face and personality, but not his name. After he paid the cab fare, Audrey Hepburn's automated voice encouraged him to, "Have a nice day!"

He approached the front desk and paid for a hotel suite with a David Kritz check, at a nightly rate of $749.99. He also left an additional $200 check as a deposit for telephone and other incidentals. The clerk passed him a gold, metal key and an additional key for the room safe. Key in hand, he asked, "Can I write you guys a check in exchange for some cash?"

"Sure, of course."

Five minutes later, he put $500 in his pocket and was left with two checks to go. God, I love this.

At 6:15 in the morning, he grabbed a taxi to West 25th to the 40-40 Lounge, the newest hot spot since the Lotus' fame faded.

Once there, an enormous line greeted him. He exited the taxi and looked for the bouncer. Kareem found him, and gave him the $500 from the Plaza front desk. He was then whisked past the line.

Kareem scanned the club. Cristall, Courvoisier, and ecstasy floated everywhere. There was a select few of the celebrity party heads up in VIP. Amidst all that debauchery, he had yet to spot Marquis and could not reach him by phone. He was tapped on the shoulder by a sexy, chocolate woman. She signaled for him to join her on the dance floor. Lil' Kim's and 50 Cents' *Magic Stick* blared through the system, so he took her up on her offer.

Later, while at the bar with his dance partner, Rochelle, he got a call from Marquis, who told him, "Meet me over at the second floor unisex bathroom, pronto."

"Aiight," he responded. He excused himself from Rochelle to make his way to the bathroom after ensuring that she would be there when he returned.

At the bathroom, he found Marquis outside with a blonde-haired Eve look-a-like. "I like your style, nigga," he told Marquis referring to Eve.

"Oh, that's just for the night. I have Asian and white blondes where that came from."

"Okay, Playa."

Marquis and Kareem chatted for a moment before Kareem told him that he had Rochelle waiting for him at the bar. Then he added, "We can roll to my hotel," picking up the lyrics of Cassidy's song that blared in the background.

Back with Rochelle, they exchanged words, but Kareem kept in mind if you're at an after-after party, you're looking to get into a one night stand. "Let's stop kidding ourselves. You fuckin'?" Kareem was bold, as he stared deep into her eyes. There was something appealing about her after a few drinks.

She eagerly replied, "You're spot or mine?"

"Mine. I'm from Philly and at the Plaza."

"Oh, the Plaza."

"Hold up I'm the catch, not the hotel."

"Don't flatter yourself, cutie"

*   *   *

At the hotel, Kareem sent Marquis to the room with the ladies and he headed for the front desk.

"Yes, I'll need to cash a check," he told the new clerk on duty.

"Sure, for how much?"

"Five hundred."

With an additional $500 in hand, Kareem headed to the room and joined the others for breakfast.

After breakfast, Marquis and Eve retreated to the bed that was toward the far side of the room. Rochelle was seated on the sofa, sipping a mimosa. Kareem sat next to her, and then he got up and dimmed the light to its lowest level. He turned on the TV and bought a rated X film. He then walked back over to Rochelle and slipped his dick into her mouth. This was why he was not pressed to fuck Toi. He whored other woman.

Like a whale eating a fish snack, she licked the head, and then licked down the entire shaft. Before long, her mouth was wrapped around his manhood. She enjoyed herself so much that she aggressively tried to devour him whole, but there was a little more than an inch that she didn't manage to swallow.

Kareem pulled her up, and they both stripped down to nothing. Rochelle got up on all fours on the edge of the bed, hungry for him to take her from behind. He tried to roughly slide his manhood into her pussy inch by inch, but she pushed back and vacuum-sucked his entire piece into her. *So, this is how she wants it!* Kareem grabbed her hips, got up on his tiptoes and dug inside of her viciously. She loved his thrusts so much that she pulled away, laid on her back with her waist hanging off the edge of the bed. He tossed her legs onto his shoulder and nailed her like a construction worker building a house from the ground up.

Next to them, Marquis had Eve on the edge of bed in doggy style. Amazingly, Eve found Rochelle's breasts in her mouth. Her tongue biting respectfully on the nipples to subdue the pain that Marquis bestowed upon her. Marquis looked at Kareem who experienced his first lesbian affair and smiled. He mouthed, "Watch this," to his best friend.

Marquis pushed Kareem back from Rochelle, and he slid out of her. His dick hung in the air for the women to admire. Marquis tapped Rochelle and told her to lay in front of Eve with her wet pussy right in her face. He pulled Rochelle hard onto his dick and demanded her to, "Eat it!"

For a few moments, Kareem watched in admiration. Wanting back in the action, he climbed on the bed and straddled over Rochelle's face, dick in her mouth. Unable to really fuck her mouth the way he wanted to, he pulled her up and slammed his dick inside of her with her legs back on his shoulders. After a considerable amount of probing, he felt Eve nibbling on his ass cheeks, before her tongue found his balls.

When Marquis was ready to explode, he threw Eve to the bed and let go all over her face. Thirsty, Eve pulled Kareem out of Rochelle and deep-throated him until her lips touched his balls. When he exploded, she got up, went to the bathroom and showered as if nothing happened.

CHAPTER 23

*T*asha's matted locks laid lovingly across Dre's chest as he awoke. The beaming sunrays blinded him as his eyes opened wider. He turned his head to shade his eyes from the sun and focused on his surroundings. Tasha's feminine fragrances scented the room, and pink walls reminded him where he was. He raised his head a little and saw the bed sheet wrapped around Tasha's curvy contours, which reminded him of how he had spent his night, and how she'll expand in a few months. What the fuck?

He laid there a moment, and thought how to deal with the baby issue with Delores. He had to tell her. She would not approve of him being a teenage father. She also would not recommend an abortion. She would, however, verbally abuse him relentlessly for that. If he failed at anything, he'd return to this defining moment. He would blame this period for all of his shortcomings and failures in life. Delores was one thing, but grandmother, Jean-Mary would be another force to reckon with. Hell, Hurricane Jeanne had nothing on Hurricane Jean-Mary.

Tasha rolled over to the unoccupied side of the bed and felt around the floor for her robe. She stood naked with the sun casting a bright light over her skin. Dre enjoyed the noon eyeful. She wrapped herself with the robe and sat back on the bed. Dre rolled over and wrapped his arms around her, resting his hands on her tummy. Tasha stood and pulled Dre's hands, holding it as they walked to the shower.

Dre was glad that Tasha lived in her parents' basement, with a private entrance and shower. After the shower, Dre dressed and Tasha asked what he wanted for breakfast.

"You don't have to cook. Where you tryinna eat at?"

"Wherever you take me. As long as we can discuss what we're going to do about this," she said, rubbing her stomach.

"Okay, Tasha! If you insist on going there today, right now, fine."

Tasha huffed. "You know what, let me take you home. I'll deal with my baby alone. Maybe I'll die or have a miscarriage from the stress that you're putting me through."

Dre grabbed her tight as she began to shed tears. He tried to hold her, but she pulled away with violence.

"What do you want me to do, have an abortion? You're always talking about being there for me, and calling me your queen, but you're not showing me any love right now, and I really need you. I can't go through this alone, but I will. If you don't want me or my baby, you can leave and never say shit to me again."

CHAPTER 24

"*R*oom service," whispered a sweet voice as she knocked on the hotel room door.

"Sorry, I'm running late. I'll be ready in half an hour," Kareem said loudly. He rolled over and looked at the alarm clock. It was 3:15. Marquis got up and skidded to the bathroom, while Kareem called room service and had breakfast sent up. Kareem then dashed down to the gift shop to purchase underclothes and fresh clothing for Marquis. He billed the items to the room, and kept his cash in his pocket. After they dressed and had breakfast, they gathered their belongings and left out the room.

At the front desk, Kareem told the clerk, "I'm checking out of room 615."

"You're sorta late. Late night, Mr. Kritz?"

"Of course," Kareem replied smiling. "Spent all of my cash, too. I'd like to cash a check."

* * *

*R*ather than hop in a taxi and head back to Philadelphia, Kareem and Marquis strolled across the street from the hotel to Bergdorf Goodman. They went directly to the third floor men's street wear department and found themselves engulfed in high fashion. That level also housed the executive offices, where Kareem opened an instant credit charge account in the name of his alter ego: David Kritz. He was approved for a $3,000 line of credit.

Kareem had the intention to max out the $3,000 limit. He grabbed a mocha-colored, short-sleeve, cowhide vest, and a crocodile frock coat, both by designed Gucci. The coat cost $3,200, and the vest was $700. With the tax, he looked at a $4,200 purchase.

Before he located a salesman, he asked Marquis, "Are you getting anything?"

"No, I bought everything that I wanted from here a week ago."

"Do you have your book on you?"

"Never leave home without it. And I'm shocked that you don't have yours."

"Well, I was taken out of the bed at two, so I had to rush to the train station, remember? And I used all of the checks that I did have getting cash from the hotel."

Despite all of the debating, Kareem left the couture department store with the signature gray garment bag in hand, thanks to Marquis writing a bad check, for the balance minus the $3,000.

* * *

*D*re and Tasha enjoyed brunch at the Brew Moon when he received a phone call interrupting them. He looked at the caller ID and immediately jumped up from the table to take the call from Brent.

Brent needed Dre to handle another run for him. Dre expressed that he was having brunch with Tasha and if he abruptly left that she would suspect that he was cheating on her, especially after the night before. He did not want her jealousy to creep center stage and she began to snoop into his business and find that he was cheating on her with a possible trip to jail.

He went back to the table and informed Tasha that they would have to get their food to go. Surprisingly, she did not complain. He thought that was strange, but what was stranger was that Brent wanted him to make a special delivery to a city councilman allegedly on the payroll. A delivery that he accepted, and charged $2,000 to make.

* * *

"The rest of the day is on me, since you're not ready for the big Apple!"

"No, the big Apple is not ready for me, actually. The apple should be lucky that I am not taking a big bite today. But I have to wrap up this excursion before that 7:10 train leaves Penn Station."

They left Bergdorf's and made their way down Fifth Avenue, passing many boutiques until they reached the Prada store. Prada was Kareem's favorite designer. There he bought a linen suit, two book bags, and a laptop carrier. The laptop's cover was silver and had the signature red stripe down the side. It would be quite the classroom accessory for Toi, that summer at Columbia University.

They strolled two doors down to Fendi, and Kareem bought an icon printed sweater, jeans, and a day planner. They crossed Fifth Avenue and went to Gucci, Marquise's favorite designer. With his career in mind, Kareem bought four ties, two suits, and a briefcase.

At 6:15, Kareem realized that he would never make it to Penn Station to catch his train. So, the fraudulent two hopped into a taxi and had a change of plans. Marquis called Continental Airlines.

When the airline took him off hold, Marquis became Norris Vanderbilt. He purchased an electronic ticket for is nephew, David Kritz, whom was stranded in New York City, with the true Mr. Vanderbilt's Mastercard. Confirmation in hand, Marquise paid the taxi driver a $50 tip, and Kareem made his trip to JFK Airport in record time.

* * *

Kareem boarded flight 621, seated in first class and relaxed. He was sat next to the fashion editor of *GQ*. Kareem had read all of the editor's articles over the past two years.

Politely, Kareem said, "How are you, Mr. Ritter?"

"Fine. You have to be an avid reader of the rag. And so young."

"Actually, at sixteen, I'm more than an avid reader. I have been influenced by the magazine. When I entered high school two years ago, I wanted to be a litigator, but after reading GQ, I am going to Columbia this summer to study fashion design."

"Oh, that's great," Mr. Ritter said surprised. "I was sure that we influenced men's style, but not altered career choices."

That probe continued throughout the flight and ended with Mr. Ritter passing along his business card. He said, "You seem like the perfect candidate for an internship. Assuming you're interested, call me when you begin CU."

* * *

The eleven o'clock news began, and Brent called Bob McNeil and confirmed that the package delivery to Councilman Adams had been done. Brent sounded as if he kissed ass, in an effort to impress the man that had supplied him with the cash to pursue his drug dealing aspirations.

"You sent the black kid, right?" Bob asked and knew the answer. "Don't need your hands dirty." He had watched Dre deliver the package. "We had to get rid of that little problem."

"What problem is Adams going to get us out? He's constantly sending cops to my spots."

Brent had annoyed Bob to the maximum degree. Bob was amazed that young men feared and followed the idiot. "Look here, son, Adams was the problem. Turn on the news to see how I handle problems."

The newscaster reported a breaking story. The caster said: "Right now details are sketchy, but we do know that Councilman Franklin Adams had been poisoned. Medical examiners believe that Adams appears to have indulged in abusing cocaine and received a very bad batch. The drugs have been recovered and are being tested..."

"Bob, tell me that I did not have a councilman killed?"

"Oh! I'm Bob now. Listen you little puppet. You'll do as I tell you. Otherwise you can kiss this life goodbye. The Illegal Gratuity Act makes it a criminal offense for anyone to give anything of value to a public official. In this case it was illicit drugs. Need I say more?" Bob let that sink in and then, he said, "Now you just keep that nigger in check, and the money will continue to pour in."

* * *

Dre watched the news broadcast and was devastated that he was responsible for conspiring to kill a councilman. He laid back on his bed and brood where he went from that point. He was a drug dealer, a murderer, and a high school student, all by seventeen. *I've done a great fucking job, so far*, he thought sarcastically. *I'll be in jail for life, just like my stupid fucking father. But I am not going out like a clown-joker, like dear old dad, though.*

He rolled over and called Chino, and vowed to rid himself of Brent.

PART TWO

JUNE 2003
(Six Months Later)

CHAPTER 25

It was June and the Bezel brothers had graduated from Upper Merion and they both lived on their own. The paper hangar was in New York City as planned, but the drug dealer had moved to Bensalem, another Philadelphia suburb. Dre needed to be away from where he sold drugs to be with Tasha and raise their baby in peace.

Dre gave Chino his hand to shake, and asked him what was good.

"I'm good. Just trying to come up. My connect acting all crazy, 'cause some of his young bulls got knocked by the feds. He fucks up my money by not breaking me off."

Dre knew that was an opportunity to begin getting rid of all the drugs that he had in the tuck from copping for BG. He and Chino took a stroll around that largely Puerto Rican Bad Lands, and negotiated a deal that would get them both paid. Dre was straight up with Chino, but he didn't reveal that he was the supplier and not Ice, as he had told Chino. It was business, and Dre did not want his friendship with Chino to get into the way of his profit. A profit that he had patiently waited to make.

Dre had wanted to get into the Latino loop, so that he could blowup. Chino was in the position to put Dre onto some real dollars.

With his deal sealed, Dre pulled off in his Camry, a graduation gift from Eli. He did not want to be in the Bad Lands any longer than necessary. The last thing that he needed was the federal agents on his top. Despite the shock that he would be a father, he continued to prepare for the baby's arrival and this deal was a part of that preparation. With other business to attend, he smiled at the idea of fatherhood and sped off.

Dre drove down Hunting Park Avenue and his cell phone rang. It was Tasha.

Without preamble, she said, "Dre, ever since we moved together, I see less and less of you. This is not what I planned…"

Tasha had felt lonely and neglected. Dre continued to assure her that, she was always on his mind. He had to be in the streets hustling to keep the roof over their heads, though. His post office gig barely paid half the bills. He told her that he would be in and then disconnected the call. He did not want to turn the conversation into a nightmare.

CHAPTER 26

"Toi, I have to go. If you were my employer, how would you like me showing up late on my first day?"

"Well as sexy as you are, I'd probably listen to your explanation and give you a pass. You would not do it again, though."

"Cute, but you're not the boss. I am leaving this dorm, now." Kareem kissed her passionately and within seconds he had second thoughts about being to work on time. He had plenty of money and did not need a job. He wanted to ravish her sexually. He was patient with her being a virgin, as he knew that New York would turn her into a sex pot.

Kareem exited the dorm room and hopped into a taxi. Life was on track. First summer semester in college, in one of the top cities in the world for advancement. He had passed eight SAT II exams, and shaved 24-credits from his pursuit to earning a Bachelor of Arts degree. He also had an eighteen credit course load and a part time gig at Chemical Bank. The track had a fast train on it.

Laura Masters, the bank manager, greeted Kareem when he arrived to his new job. "Glad you made it," she told him smiling.

Don't know how bad I almost did not to make it, Kareem thought. "New York traffic is amazing. I had to take a taxi and then abandon it, for the train."

"This is NY; such is life, but call if you think you're going to be late. Let me give you the tour, and the get you set up with Beth McAllister for training."

After he was shown around, Laura introduced Kareem to Beth. The two shook hands and settled into his office. Beth was beautiful—a twenty on a scale of 1-10. He imagined getting into her tight little Chanel skirt.

"Go ahead, Mr. Bezel, take a seat. It is yours."

Boy is she sweet. I can taste her perfume, he thought. Toi would have to lose her virginity soon, before he went and did something crazy like have an affair at the job.

Rather than take a seat, Kareem pulled Beth close to him with one arm and yanked her hair with the other. "I can see in your eyes that you want me to fuck you."

Beth simply mustered, "Ummmm. Oh! Um," as he lifted her skirt up and pulled her panties down.

He spun her around, and with his best Billy Dee Williams impression, he smoothly told her, "Bend over and grab your ankles, Beth." She complied and he slid deep into her guts from the back. He dug into her quickly and violently. He knew that they were pressed for time. Just as he was about to climax, he heard a finger snap.

"Mr. Bezel," Beth said. "Snap out of it. Is this your first office?"

"Uh—yes. Just caught up in a thought. Sorry. Where were we?" He prayed that she did not observe his erection.

* * *

After work, Kareem stopped at the Cartier shop. When greeted by the salesman, he expressed his desire for a gold-plated pen, and possibly a credenza to decorate his office.

"Really," the salesman responded. "Well, where do you work?"

"Saatchi and Saatchi." Kareem lied. Saatchi was a top New York advertising firm, usually responsible for the biggest Super Bowl commercials.

"Oh, in that case, I have the perfect décor. One of the top execs of the firm was here an hour ago."

Kareem loved when the plan came together. He said, "So, you have instructions to bill everything to the Saatchi account?"

"Sure do," the salesman replied joyously. "Follow me."

* * *

Nine-thousand-dollars was charged to the Saatchi account to buy a credenza, desk calendar, two gold desk picture frames, a pen holder, tape holder, briefcase, and two 14-karat gold pens.

Back at his dorm, the smooth criminal called Jean-Mary to see how she was doing.

She asked him, "How was your first day at work?"

"Lovely. I also picked out a condo."

"So, when am I coming to visit?"

"Give me a month, or two to decorate and I'm going to invite the entire family up. I do not want any jealously."

"Yeah, I hear you," she replied. Jean-Mary was very familiar with Kareem's maternal family being jealous of their bond. What they did not understand was that they all had each other and all Jean-Mary had was Kareem, despite her having five living children, other than the arrested James Bezel.

They chit-chatted for a while, and he told her, "I was just checking in on you. I'll call you later."

"Okay. Behave, baby."

"Impossible," he replied smiling, and hung up.

CHAPTER 27

AUGUST 2003 (Two Months Later)

"*These last two months have been quite amazing, don't you think?*" Kareem asked Toi, as he drove down Madison Avenue to the Kill Bill movie premiere.

Toi sat in silence, though. Kareem just kept talking. He said, "I'll bet we both get 4.0 GPA's after we turn in our final projects and take the exams. We are about to blow up." Toi continued her silence. "Toi!" he yelled out, and cut the music.

"What?" she responded angrily.

"What's with the silent treatment?" he asked, and pulled the car over into a fire lane. He was pissed.

"You have to excuse me, Kareem Bezel, if I am not impressed with the way that you have been neglecting me."

"You have to be kidding?" he asked, pulling into the traffic. He then reminded her, "I have an eighteen credit course load. I work four nights a week at the bank. I intern at *GQ* twice a week. I try to spend all of the rest of my time with you when I am not studying. My career has us attending a movie premiere with the A-list..."

"Maybe that's the problem. Maybe, I am not contributing to this relationship."

"What the hell are you talking about? We're young and in love, living 100-miles away from anyone else that we know and love. I'm having the time of my life. I thought as partners that you were in the boat with me. Are you jumping ship? We have not gotten anywhere."

"Maybe, I'm not ready for all of this."

"What's with the maybe shit? You know what, let's go home!"

CHAPTER 28

That weekend, Kareem and Toi took their first visit to Philadelphia. After they visited both of their parents, they headed over to Dre and Tasha's place to see what they had been up to. Kareem could tell by the décor of the pad and Tasha's new Audi that, Dre was heavy in the drug game.

BG had Dre cop kilograms of cocaine and heroine for him. Dre had also been making his own sales, covering a wider range of drugs (pills and syrup). His reputation as a drug dealer had spread around the suburbs. Dre was the main supplier of the types of drugs that attracted young, white kids, and the man fronting BG money did not like that.

Dre also dealt with some personal worries. He had begun to question his genuine love for Tasha and oftentimes thought about leaving her. She picked arguments with him for no reason, and Dre could no longer take it. He hung in there for his son's sake, but it was only a matter of time before he would be forced to leave her.

"Dre, can you change Amare's diaper?" Tasha asked, as she prepared to go to the gym in an effort to attack the baby fat. She was anxious to get her figure back, after she delivered, Amare Bezel and his six pounds, eight ounces, three weeks earlier.

"Of course, I can't." Dre joked, showing off in front of his little brother.

"Come on, I'm trying to get dressed. You're such a showoff," Tasha said. She was tired of his shit, too.

"You two are hilarious. That's why I know that I am not having a baby anytime soon." Toi blurted out.

"Calm that shit down. I was joking," Dre said, looking directly at Toi's stuck up ass. "And virgins can't get pregnant. I thought that you were the hell smart."

"Boy, you were about to get knocked out by your girl, so don't talk shit to me," Toi said jokingly, and gave Tasha a high five.

"I'll be glad when you heal up, so I can knock you out. Then my son will grow up and do the same to his women: knock them up and down."

"Your son will not be like you," Kareem said.

Be like me! What the fuck that was supposed to mean? Dre thought, but he already knew. "With these brown eyes like his dad, he'll be pulling grown ass women in the pee-wee leagues."

Dre put Amare in his crib with a pacifier in his mouth, and then looked into a Timberland box where he kept his current stash of $47,000. He also had a safe in the event that someone dared to be foolish enough to break into the apartment. He planned to show them the dummy safe and then make every effort to kill them. Dre was reckless and had become a monster. At the post office, he had poked a co-worker in the head three times for bumping into him without saying anything along the lines of an apology. Luckily, Dre was not the flashy type, or he would either be broke or hustling harder, putting himself further into the danger zone of arrest and kissing Tasha and his son goodbye.

Dre heard a knock at the door, and yelled, "I'll get it," before anyone else attempted to answer it. At the door, he asked who was there, and to his surprise the visitor claimed to be a Drug Enforcement Administration Agent.

"May, I help you," Dre asked cautiously. He opened the door and stepped out.

"Yes, I am Drug Enforcement Agent Lucas McKenzey. I'd like to have a chat with you."

"I don't chat with agents."

"Oh! We can chat at my office, which would be better for me. Your choice, though," the agent said, wearing an expression of amusement on his face.

Dre knew that the man was in charge, so he decided to step outside to keep everybody out of his business, especially Kareem. He had no desire to give Kareem any more ammunition.

"So, how can I help you mister, huh…?"

"You have not missed anything," McKenzey said, contemptuously. "It's Agent McKenzey. At any rate, what's your involvement with Brent Gower? Your boy BG."

"There is no involvement."

"Sure there is, or was."

"Right. He was a former teammate that I won the state championship with," Dre said matter-of-factly. It was as if, he did not have a care in the world.

The agent knew better, though.

"What's your current involvement with his drug sales?"

"Funny dude you are."

"There is an involvement, I know that. And I want to know who continues to supply BG with the cash to operate?" the agent asked. He pulled out a portable DVD player and showed Dre make his first pick-up at the mall parking lot. And his later phone call from the bank parking lot pay phone.

Dre hid his amazement. "Arrest me, then. I ain't talking."

"Don't need to, I know. Just tell me who gives the kid money to stay afloat."

"I ain't talking. Did you hear me?"

"Somehow, I knew that you would not want to be interested in beating BG to the grand jury. He will be there, because he hates your kind, and won't hesitate to fry you."

"Good. Am I under arrest?"

"No."

"Have a nice one," Dre said and spun back into the apartment.

"Who was that?" Kareem asked.

"It was a college scout," Dre replied, and wished that Kareem was not there. He grabbed Tasha and told her, "I told him that I have a wife and a son, and I don't plan on going away."

Dre had to get up much earlier to fool Kareem, though. He did not know what the man was there for then, but he vowed to find out.

* * *

Agent McKenzey hopped into his vehicle and smiled. He knew exactly who was providing BG with the cash to buy drugs. He just wanted to make sure that Dre had not known that it was him, Agent McKenzey all along McKenzey was pissed that Dre was no longer dealing with BG, which slowed down his corrupt profits. And for that, Andre Bezel would pay. That day was a warning shot.

CHAPTER 29

*K*areem's alarm clock blared, awakening him and his dorm mate. He had possession of the keys to his Upper Eastside digs, but he was strictly forbidden to live off campus for the summer session. Kareem was glad that he was awake because the nightmare that he had had frightened him. He could not believe that the man that visited Dre was the same man that had handed BG money to give to Dre moments before Dre arrived to the Sears parking lot. Kareem wished that Dre hadn't taken the visitor outside, so that he could have heard the conversation. He popped the security video that he swiped from the mall security office into his VCR to be sure that the man at Dre's apartment and the man in the video were the same, for the tenth time. He began to wonder was the man a cop? A co-conspirator? Or was he a complete fraud? Kareem knew precisely what to do to find out who the man was. He called, Ravonne Lemmelle, cousin and attorney at law.

Kareem wrapped up his call and decided that he needed to get out and play a while. All summer he had been stuck on campus and bound by a 2 a.m. curfew. It had been hectic, but he would make up for the lost time during the two week break coming up. He would also move out of the dorm and, against his better judgment, take Toi with him to co-habitate.

The rules of the dorm had an advantage, though. He worked on opening his clothing store, and launching his clothing line. He sketched quite a few pieces to present, Bjorn Prodigy to the world, and make it a household name in a decade. He even had developed the company's motto: Many men are born. Few are Bjorn Prodigy.

His debut men's wear line would take high-fashion street wear to a whole new level.

After he showered, he left the dorm room and hailed a taxi. He was eager to get to GQ. Each year the magazine honored the "Woman of the Year" and that year it was Donatella Versace, for her edgy new gothic "DV" line. In the taxi, he called his brother, and when the phone was picked up, he heard Amare screaming.

"Why is he screaming like that? Does he want to be breast fed? You two better not be torturing my nephew. Where's Dre?" He asked laughing.

Dre had already picked up the other phone, and said, "What's good?" He was chuckling, but said, "Don't mention breast to my girl. Her titties are sore."

"From you, or the baby? Better not be forcing him to watch you fuck her, either. Listen, I am going to the Victoria Secret's yearly fashion show tonight. You have to come up now, if you wanna go.

"Damn, I'm busy tonight. I gotta pass."

Kareem knew what kind of business that Dre had to handle and he wanted to tell his brother to get out of the game, but he knew that Dre was stuck. He told him, "I have tickets to a Tyra after party. You can't pass up on that."

"Naw, I can't, homey. Wish that I could."

"You're a lame." Kareem barked and hung up.

* * *

Kareem stared at a huge work load when he had the receptionist put Toi through.

"Kareem, I know you are busy..."

"That's why my cell is off."

"And that is why I have the office number." She snapped back. "The contractors called and wanted to know what color you want the kitchen. Apparently, they are just getting around to handling the jobs that you requested, because they procrastinated since they knew you had to live on campus."

"Tell them very light green."

"Light green will be sexy with a paisley print of green, black, and silver."

"Sounds cool. I have to go, though."

"O...Kay," she said, softly. She hated when she was second to his job. *GQ was not even a job, it was an internship for crying out loud*, she thought. Something that he could quit as far as she was concerned. "I love you."

"Ditto!"

"Ditto, my ass. I love you."

"I love you, too, Toi."

Without a reply she hung up.

CHAPTER 30

*L*ater that night, Dre arrived at the Palmer Social Club. And despite the long line, he was whisked to the VIP door and carted off to the elite section. Allen Iverson sat across from him, as well as Lloyd Banks, who promoted his new CD. Dre became bored quickly with the fake-ass celebrities, so he headed to the "regular" club hoppers bar area, because he was regular no matter how much money he had in the tuck.

At the bar, he ordered a Thug Passion—a drink mix of Red Passion Alize and Hennessy—to mellow him out. Dre gave the bar maid a Benjamin and told her to run him a tab. After several drinks and several chicken heads trying to get is attention, he eyed a caramel model-esque woman with her hair in a short wrap.

Courvoisier in one hand, shot glass in the other, Dre walked to the woman who bounced her head to the music. He prepared to lay his game down on her, so that later that night, he could lay his pipe down on her. He wondered where BG was, so that he could get out of there.

After five songs on the dance floor, four shots, no sign of BG, and Dre and Leah telling a bunch of lies to each other, they left the club to head to the Marriott Hotel on the corner of 13th and Market Streets.

They exited the club, arms locked, as they walked toward Dre's car. Dre wondered why BG didn't meet him as planned to discuss a proposed blockbuster deal. BG had him down that corny-ass club knowing that he was not going to show. Dre was furious. Had he not grabbed a piece of ass for the night, Dre may have gone and blew up BG's spot. Dre had become increasingly short-tempered over the past year.

Dre opened the passenger door to let Leah in and an unknown thug poked Dre in the head with a gun, and mumbled, "Run that shit in, before I blow you and the bitch top!"

Dre used his streetwise acuity and pushed Leah hard to the ground, as he quickly spun around and grabbed the potential bandit's arm. They wrestled for the gun, and Leah crawled to her car that was parked in the cul-de-sac.

Leah managed to get her car key into her door despite her delirium. She was a little bruised from the force that Dre used to protect her. Just as she closed her car door, she heard a loud sound resembling a textbook hitting the floor at ten miles per hour. She quickly locked her car door and watched incredulously.

Another tall guy with a Desert Eagle had slapped Dre in his head. Dre immediately let go of the goon that he struggled with. A third thug held Dre at gunpoint with a gun so big, it was described as made for TV. The first bandit Dre had wrestled with pushed him against his car, splattering his blood all over the front passenger window. Another took Dre's gun from his waistband.

Dre was angry. Through all the wrestling, he never had the opportunity to retrieve his own gun. A goon backhand-slapped Dre like a hoe on her knees giving bad head. And then another dude searched Dre's pockets, and then his car for cash or valuables.

Upset that the car was empty, the attacker aggressively asked, "Where the fuck is the shit at," while he gripped Dre by the collar.

"What shit?" Dre answered the farcical question dumbfounded. He could not believe those lame-ass project dwellers from behind the club tried to rob him. Dre was smart enough not to bring any drugs or money to the club, even though, BG expected him to bring cash. They had had to settle for the $200 play money that he had left over after drinks and shit. In an instant, Dre had received another blow to the head.

"You want to play fucking games, Dre," the thug seethed.

Dre's head rang loudly, and he could not believe the dude knew his name.

The man then ordered another thug to, "Flatten his fucking tires!"

Dre sat silent and watched his tires slashed by some sort of jackknife. The hiss was loud, and Dre was surrounded by snakes in the grass.

The thugs all jumped into an all too familiar Dodge Charger, and left Dre with a searing insult.

* * *

Dre grabbed his cell phone and called Tasha. After the phone rang four times, the answering machine picked up. Dre dialed right back. He was worried that the men had been to his apartment, or was on their way there.

"Hello," Tasha said with a soft voice, trying to disguise her I-was-sleep-voice.

Dre on the other hand was hyped. "Tasha get up, and take Amare to my grand mom Jean-Mary's now!"

"Boy, what are you..."

"Tasha!! He barked. "Get the fuck up, and do the fuck what I just said. Get yourself up and my boy, and go to my G mom's now!" He hollered into the phone. He sounded draconian, but that was what Tasha asked for.

He hung up and Leah pulled next to him. He hopped into her car, and they hastily drove to Hahnemann University Hospital at Broad and Vine Streets.

* * *

Bob McNeil had sat in his car and used binoculars to watch Dre be handled. He laughed hysterically, as he watched the assault on the black man unfold as he planned it to. He had rap music—Tupac—blasting in the background, as he sipped an Old English from the bottle.

He loved to see his orders carried out. After all, it was his money invested there. Bob had no intention of letting Dre or BG get over on him. He could not have that. A kid out witting him, never! He was smarter than both of them. More importantly, he was Drug Enforcement Agent Lucas McKenzey, and his puppet BG didn't even know it.

CHAPTER 31

*D*re received stitches in two separate areas of his head. He had a lot on his *mind.* In the last year, or so, his life he had gone from a high school student, to a father, a drug dealer, and a postal worker. Now, he had to add murderer to his credentials.

Outside of the emergency room doors, Dre tapped Leah on her shoulder to awake her. They then walked out to her Chrysler 300C, and Dre stood in front of her.

He looked her square in her eyes and thanked her for sticking around. "I truly apologize for tonight's bullshit." He was sincere.

"What was that all about?" Leah asked. She was curious.

He put an index finger to her lips. "Let's not worry about that. That's all behind us as of right now. Deal?"

Leah nodded, and Dre continued. "Let's exchange numbers and I'll treat you to dinner." He removed his finger and Leah was starry eyed as if she had met her knight. After all, she felt like he had saved her from any abuse from the thugs.

"Dinner sounds great. As long as there isn't any shooting," she said and smiled, looking him deep into his eyes, twirling her hair with her finger.

"Sounds good," he said. "I should let you go; you've been up long enough. Drive safely."

"You don't need a ride home?" Leah asked. She sounded like she wanted Dre's company for the night.

"No, I'll be fine. Thanks," Dre said and turned to walk away, but he was stopped.

"Wait! You forgot my number." Leah yelled out.

She had stroked his ego. That was a little trick, he had learned from his dad. Dre turned around and wrapped his arms around Lisa and accompanied her home.

* * *

*D*re arrived at Leah's apartment and wondered what she did for a living. Her home was luxurious.

She went to the kitchen and poured Dre a drink. When she returned, Dre was on her sofa with his eyes shut, shaking his leg uncontrollably. Leah sat the glass of water on a coaster on the end table and lustfully stared at Dre. She went into her storage closet, grabbed an expensive quilt and wrapped Dre in it. She then went into her bedroom understanding that he needed to be left alone to think.

When Dre heard Leah close her bedroom door, he opened his eyes and thought, *damn.* He had a bad bitch that stayed by him just a few feet away as the drama unfolded. And yet, he had no desire to have sex with her. His blood was boiling and he could not think straight. He would fall back that night and get her another time. The good thing was, he would smoothly tell her how much he respected her not to have sex with her on the first night. He smiled at the charming analysis. He liked that she was sensitive to his situation and didn't leave him for dead, or call the police. It was best that the police did not arrive. He adored her for that, because he planned to get the clowns that fucked with him.

Dre lay for a few minutes, but he could not sleep. The anger consumed him. He thought of a masterful plan to return the favor to Brent Gower and the sorry King of Prussia gang that he headed. After he wreaked his brain for two hours, he finally nodded off.

* * *

That morning at about 7:30, Dre crept out of Leah's apartment, and left a note on her refrigerator. He walked to Broad Street and hailed a taxi to take him to meet the tow man at his car.

After the tow man changed all of his tires, Dre sped up I-95 and headed to his pad. He found his apartment ransacked and knew who was responsible. He was glad that Tasha had listened to him and he did not find her and their son harmed, or worse dead. Tasha was a tough woman, though. She was trained to fend off an attacker with the pistol that Dre had bought her.

He assessed the situation, and then he called Chino to control the damage.

Chino answered, and Dre said, "I need you at my crib tonight. I'll tell you why when you get here."

"No doubt, I'm there," Chino said. He had detected violence and wanted parts.

Dre hung up and then called BG, who answered the phone with a surprised tone. Dre did not know if it was because he was shocked that he was not dead, or astonished that Dre had the balls to call him.

In a condescending state, Dre used his most placid tone to mask his anger. "Listen, BG, I totally apologize for crossing you. That won't happen again. I know you had a lot of respect for me and you lost that, maybe, but, you know that I rely heavily on your drug runs to maintain my lifestyle." He lied. "So, with that apology out the way, I'd like to still meet you tonight to handle business,"

BG was not surprised at how submissive Dre had suddenly become after the beat down. Bob McNeil had told BG that the attack would humble Dre and he would stop stepping on his toes. Bob was right. BG felt gratified that he had Dre right where he wanted him.

* * *

Right on schedule, Dre was in the AMC theater parking lot at the Neshaminy Mall. Dre and Chino waited in Dre's car, and Dre was glad that this was the last time that he would meet up with BG. Dre always knew that his drug career had to end, but he planned to get out after he sparked that clown.

Avery, BG's lieutenant, walked toward Dre's car, and Dre jumped out before Avery was up on it. Dre thought that he had been out smarted by BG, by him sending a proxy as opposed to him showing his face.

When Avery and Dre was faced to face, Avery explained, "There's $98,000 here," as he handed over a duffle bag. "BG wants four big boys. Keep the change."

Dre ignored that. "Why did he send you? I do not do business with his hired help."

"Hired help! Didn't I teach you a lesson last night, faggot?" Avery asked, leaning into Dre to add an intimidating effect with his comment, and pointed a finger into his chest.

Dre smiled as he watched Chino creep up behind Avery and used his .44 Bulldog to smack Avery in the head.

With blood gushing everywhere, Chino had Avery at gunpoint. "Lemme kill this pussy right now, Dre."

Dre turned around and walked away. The light wind forced his jacket to flutter. The silence was cut by two shots. Within seconds, Dre heard Chino's foot steps behind him. Chino threw the duffle bag with Brent's cash into the back seat of the car and anxiously, asked Dre, "Can we go get that sucka BG, now?"

* * *

Dre returned to his apartment and told Chino to take $50,000 out the duffle bag, for handling his business. Chino then left after he assured Dre that if he needed anything handled that he should call him to take care of it. Dre sat back, turned on the TV and contemplated his next move. He had to get BG. The Eagles had lost and that was fine. But the breaking news about the young, white male left dead in the mall parking lot was not.

And Dre whipped into action.

CHAPTER 32

Hours later, Dre was knee deep in a porcelain tub full of suds at a hotel in Wilmington, Delaware. He relaxed in the Jacuzzi because he could not sleep. Regret had consumed him, but not enough to march to the police station and accept responsibility for the death of Avery Snobli.

Out of the tub, he was forced to listen to new casters plead for anyone with information regarding the shooting at the Neshaminy Mall to come forward. The news caster also claimed that the police had a suspect in mind. At that instant, Dre panicked. *Could they be on to me? Did BG rat on me?* Those things played in Dre's head. He decided to call the only person with the ability to improve his situation. Surely Kareem would have some advice. Too bad Dre hadn't listened to Kareem's earlier advice: Never do a deal in a mall parking lot!

"Kareem, I am in trouble," he told his younger brother, urgently. Kareem was the smarter brother and Dre knew that, and was not ashamed to admit it. "I cannot talk to you over the phone, though. Meet me at the Wilmington Amtrak station at eleven a.m. Your train leaves at 8:26, this morning. I already checked." Dre was very direct with his request and hoped that his brother complied without a fight.

"Let me book a seat."

"Already done. Business class, too, 'cause you a stuck-up-ass nigga," he said chuckling.

*   *   *

Kareem arrived at the Wilmington train station and could not find his brother. After five minutes of pacing and several glances at his watch, he was approached by a woman completely concealed in Muslin garb. "Kareem, it's me."

Kareem looked down at the ground and shook his head in disbelief. He said, "You make a lovely woman, and I didn't even see your face."

"I do. And I am ready for jihad."

When they arrived to the hotel, Dre came out of drag and took Kareem to the scene of the crime. He told him every detail. To which Kareem calmly replied: "Don't worry, I'll get you out of this mess."

"And how the fuck you gonna do that, smart-ass-nigga." Dre could not believe that his brother was being so nonchalant.

"Listen, I have some things to do that I can't tell you. You gotta trust me. Your little brother."

*   *   *

Later that day, the brothers arrived at Jean-Mary's. Dre hugged Tasha and felt on her booty, he needed that. Everyone was glad that he was fine, but Jean-Mary was concerned with why Kareem was not in New York finishing his exams. He explained that he was finished, and then told Dre to relax.

"Lemme put my plan into effect," were his words before he left the house.

CHAPTER 33

A task force that consisted of seven full time officers was formed to crack the Avery Snobli murder case. E-mail and private telephone lines allowed hundreds of leads to pour into the Neshaminy police station. None of the calls identified the killer, though.

The medical examiner's report stated that there was a two-inch hematoma contusion in Snobli's temporal lobe, along with one .25 caliber shell casing.

At the crime scene, investigators found a credit card receipt from a nearby gas station under the body. Video surveillance from the Mobile gas station produced no credible leads. The credit card owner had bought gas. Through an interview, the grandmother whose card it was, was dismissed as a suspect, considering she had been taking her grandchildren to the movies and she had no motive to kill Snobli.

"McKenzey, there's a call on line one for you," yelled a cranky duty officer, whom was tired of taking calls.

"McKenzey," he answered in a business like manner. After listening to the caller a few moments, DEA Agent, Lucas McKenzey scrambled to find a pen to write down the informant's information. After a ten minute probe, he disconnected from the tipster.

"Andre Bezel commited the murder. Black male, from King of Prussia. According to the source, he is at his grandmother's hiding in Philadelphia."

* * *

*A*bout an hour later, Jean-Mary heard an insistent banging on her front door. She scrambled to it, all ready to curse out the inconsiderate jerk that acted like a policeman. She opened the front door and did a double take when she saw a white man in a suit. He was backed up by four uniformed officers with their guns drawn.

"We need Andre Jamel Bezel at once."

Jean-Mary calmly asked, "Sir, do you have a warrant?" She had learned from Dope's arrest to never allow the cops into her home lacking a warrant.

"Well, no…"

McKenzey could not finish his statement because Jean-Mary had begun to close the door in his face. It was a bold move considering the guns. McKenzey countered by pushing open the door, knocking her to the floor, as he and the other officers penetrated the home.

The cops immediately encountered Tasha, who they commanded to sit on the sofa. Jean-Mary was helped up and ordered to the sofa, as well.

"Where is he?" McKenzey hissed, ignoring Tasha's tears.

Jean-Mary was mad as a mutha-fucka and ready to act the hell up. Dre stopped her, though.

"Hey! Police I'm coming down. Leave my peoples alone!"

McKenzey yelled for him to come down the stairs on his knees. Backwards, and crawling like an animal. Dre felt like a two-dollar-hoe, but he did it. At the bottom of the stairs, he was slammed down and frisked for a weapon.

Jean-Mary blurted out, "That was so damn unnecessary. Assholes!"

"Ma'am..."

"Ma'am my ass. You have him now get out of my house."

Dre could not believe that Kareem had turned him in. His own flesh and blood. His little brother. He was thrown into the back of a unmarked car while McKenzey gave a press conference on Jean-Mary's lawn.

* * *

Kareem looked on from a neighbor's window at his brother being hauled away. He smiled and rubbed his hands together.

CHAPTER 34

The next day, McKenzey privately questioned Cathy, his tipster, for two hours and was certain that she could identify the killer at trial. She claimed to have been at the movie theater on the night in question and that she recognized Andre Bezel from a high school football game. She had been attracted to him sexually and would not forget his face. The night before, Dre had been interrogated fiercely, and was not permitted any sleep. He was handcuffed to a chair, in a room with very bright lights, and forced to drink black coffee.

At eleven a.m. attorney, Ravonne Lemmelle, flanked by Kareem—dressed in a million-dollar suit—entered the police headquarters, prepared for a line-up. Lemmelle, one of Philadelphia's newest, yet most popular attorney's was prepared to have his client and cousin released. Kareem was by his side posing as a legal assistant.

Tension filled the air in the line-up room, a small space outfitted with TV cameras ready to roll, TV/VCR combos, and a two-inch-thick, one-way glass window through which the witnesses identified suspects. Kareem, Lemmelle, Agent McKenzey, Bensalem Township Police Chief Esche, and Assistant United States Attorney Barnswell all took seats. Cathy was then escorted into the room by an officer.

Under the captain's command, Dre and four other males entered the room on the other side of the one way glass, and took their places under the numbers one through five painted on the wall.

AUSA Barnswell had an ugly half-inch scar on his face, rumored to have come from a trial defendant. He was a tall man with a face that remained evil. He had a brown mole between his eyebrows that was equally as scary as the scar. He looked at Cathy in her eyes, and told her, "Take your time. We need you to point out the man responsible for killing Avery Snobli."

"Oh, come on, Barnswell! This is being recorded. Can you be any more suggestive? She does not have to pick out someone!" Lemmelle chided. He then shot his eyes at Cathy, and said, "If you're not sure that any of them did it, say that. Do not feel pressured to send the wrong man to the electric chair." Lemmelle was the very sardonic son of the Pennsylvania Governor. He also wore his homosexuality very masculine, and that irritated all of his opponents. And some of his clients, but he had a one-hundred-percent acquittal rating, so he was highly sought and respected, regardless.

Cathy played both suggestions in her head, and then said, "I think he's number five. I'm not one-hundred-percent sure, but I will go with number five."

"Good job, Cathy." Lemmelle interjected before closing his briefcase and turning to Barnswell. "Should we still be here? She's unsure of the perp, and we both know—well, we should—that she would not make a credible *eye* witness."

"Wait! I'm really leaning on number five."

McKenzey wanted to rip her face off and put in under number one in the suspect room, right beside Dre, who was number two.

"Take your time, Cathy. Just pick out the man who resembles that murderer," McKenzey said.

"Sounds like coercion. Are we done?" Lemmelle asked. He did not play with the Government at trial, nor during tax season.

Cathy stated that she could not be sure, and McKenzey's top blew off. He placed his hands behind his head to prevent himself from reaching out to Cathy and strangling her. He asked everyone to leave the room. Everyone looked confused, because McKenzey never gave up so easily. But they all stood to leave and McKenzey said, "Mr. Bezel stay a while. Let's see what you're learning up at Columbia, my boy."

"Not your boy! More like your nightmare." Kareem shot back.

Lemmelle intervened. "Are you insane? I am not leaving him here. That is egregiously irresponsible and I won't allow."

"No, its okay," Kareem responded. "I'll talk to the Drug Enforcement Agent."

"Calm down, Lemmelle," McKenzey snapped. "I only wanted to ask him a few questions and he is not the accused, so you're not needed. So, you may be excused."

Hearing all of that the government looked around and decided to leave to allow the agent to work. They wanted a conviction. But Lemmelle intervened again.

"Maybe somewhere while you were building your bogus case against his brother, you misplaced the rules regarding the right to an attorney from Miranda v. Arizona, and the Sixth Amendment."

Kareem loved the sarcasm of his cousin, but he told Lemmelle, "I'll be just fine with the agent. I'd love to chat it up with him."

"You sound over confident. You wanna chat. Let's chat!" McKenzey then told Lemmelle, "He sounds like a big boy. Let me speak to him totally off the cuff."

"It's definitely off the record, all right. He signs no Miranda warning and you have ten minutes."

"Don't worry. I am sure he'll want me out of here in five."

"Or maybe you will," Lemmelle said. "I know that he can be quite ferocious."

Kareem was in the interview room alone with the agent, and watched him turn off all recording devices. He then sat across from Kareem.

"Here's the deal. I know that she can identify your brother. I'll make her. He'll get the death penalty, or worse LIFE. Care to have him confess for leniency."

"No! D-E-A Agent McKenzey, is that a promise?" Kareem asked, tenting his hands and staring icily at McKenzey.

McKenzey leaned across the table, inches away from Kareem's face. Kareem didn't flinch.

"Listen nigger. It's is fucking promise alright."

Kareem slid back from the wrath of the agent, whose breath reeked of coffee over shit. Kareem chuckled mockingly as he rotated the numbers on his briefcase, and unlocked it. He said to the agent, "Where'd you learn that ethical approach to interrogation, the Academy for Dummies?" He was sharp, and then slid a manila folder over to McKenzey.

Kareem then stood and paced to the one way mirror, staring at the number two where his accused brother once stood. He gave his back to the pompous agent. Without turning around, and his voice piercing the room like a bullet, he said, "I've been on to your clever trickery for some time now," the kid said. "I mean, I must admit your scheme is quite interesting." Kareem turned to face his audience, after what seemed like an eon to McKenzey.

"Where'd you get these?"

"You're the agent." Kareem sneered. "I especially like the one with the cat." He had taunted the agent with photograph's that chronicled the agent's dealings with BG. "An animal cruelty charge on top of a conspiracy to distribute kilos of cocaine will look marvelous before a grand jury sitting in the Eastern District, wouldn't you agree?"

Kareem walked back over to his briefcase and retrieved a video tape. "Do you know what this tape consists of, D-E-A Agent Lucas McKenzey? Do you? It's rather intriguing, Agent McKenzey. Shall we sneak a peak? Of course, that's why I brought them along to this little tête-à-tête."

"You want to tango? Let's tango!" McKenzey said.

"Oh, I am dancing. Just all over you." Kareem shot back.

Agent McKenzey's face brimmed with anger. He could not believe his eyes. Even the most pretentious McKenzey could not deny the contents of the tape. Had the spinning room been full of the others, they would have applauded McKenzey's stupidity, and then shamelessly stripped his credentials from his waist.

Kareem peered into McKenzey's cold eyes. Kareem was hot, though. "You're no longer laughing, Agent McKenzey." Kareem quipped. The victory consumed him, but McKenzey could not tell. The teen sat there as stiff as concrete. McKenzey's face, displayed disgrace, but he looked at Kareem respectfully. Kareem stopped the tape, and said, "There's a scene coming up that I'd rather not see again."

"What could that be?"

"Let's see. You have a pistol to BG's head, and he's on his knees with your dick in his mouth, faggot!" Kareem hissed violently. He calmed and sardonically joked, "By the way, I loved the pink panties. I am an avid fashion guru and did not know that you could afford LaPerla on your salary. Let's make this simple. I want my brother out of here now."

"I must admit, you have a lot here, but that's not my call."

"It was when you got him here. But here's my fucking call, bastard. You tell them simpletons that you convinced me to wear a wire to get a confession out of my brother." He said exactly what Lemmelle and prepared him to say. "You're going to release my brother so that I can be fitted with a wire. You will do that because, later on this tape you'll see yourself tampering with Avery's dead body. I doubt that you want Barnswell to find that out. Can you say conspiracy to commit murder? Or maybe you even forced my brother to do your dirty work. He walks and you're off to Big Sandy. Try Lemmelle if you wanna. He's my cousin. No one in my family wins arguments with him. You don't want it, buddy ol' pal."

McKenzey sat silent, and brood how Lemmelle would fry him, Matlock style. McKenzey would never give him the satisfaction. He disgustedly agreed.

Kareem stood to leave, but stopped at the door. "We have one other piece of business. You must go on television and clear my brother's name as you accused him on our grandmother's lawn."

"Hey, I didn't alert the media."

"I did, silly. Just as I called them for you to announce your complete redaction of the allegations and your deepest apology. That? Or they could air your filthy laundry. And I sent Cathy, by the way."

* * *

The private jet left the Northeast, Wings Field Airport, and Kareem finally asked, "Where are we going?" He had followed Kareem's lead until that point, but he was very curious as to what had gotten him off death row.

"Los Angeles," Kareem responded flatly.

"One more question. What happened back there?"

Kareem smiled and sipped his Cola. "Remember when my car was broken into?" Dre nodded and he went on. "On the mall's security tapes, I saw an older white man give money to BG to give to you. At first, the man was irrelevant, until that man showed up at your apartment. I had already stole the video and lied telling you that some bitch told me all about what you were doing I called Ray-Ray and he assigned one of his PIs to keep an eye on you. He found out that McKenzey was crooked, so I exposed him."

"You had me followed?"

"Naw, protected."

"So, when I called you…"

"I already knew."

"What do you have over McKenzey?"

"He's crooked and a freak."

"Huh?"

"He killed a cat and threw it at a brick wall. He made BG suck his dick at gunpoint while wearing pink panties. I got it on tape."

"So, what now since you have this all figured out, I see."

"Keep getting that fucking bread."

CHAPTER 35

*H*ow *delicious it was, the checkmate, he thought. Far more gratifying than writing* a million dollars worth of bad checks. Well, maybe not that pleasant, but Kareem felt lordly after what he had done to Agent McKenzey. He confronted his brother's oppressor with a superfluity of evidence of his own to temporarily free his brother. In order to remain free, Kareem contemplated his next score.

Kareem had checked into the Grafton on Sunset Hotel and took off the suit that he had worn. He sat on top of the cooling system that protruded from under the windowpane and stared at the sky. Fifties blues played through the radio.

Dre was in the Jacuzzi and thought heavily about his brother's infallibility. He had no idea what he was going to do after the sojourn in Los Angeles. Everything seemed ethereal. Kareem had been an unobtrusive sentry, and he needed to show that he appreciated his brother's beautiful mind.

Kareem, despite his worries, did not want to bask in the victory. He banged on the bathroom door, and startled Dre. "Get the fuck out of the tub. You're not auditioning for an Oil of Olay commercial."

"For what? You have me up in this fancy ass hotel and I'm going to live it up, like a rock star."

"Look, I need you to get out, so that we can do a little shopping before we hit the club. I have to find a shot of ass for the night."

"Ass? Did you say ass? I'll be right out."

Before Kareem headed out of the hotel, he called Jean-Mary and informed her that they were fine. A short cab ride from the hotel and the two brothers entered Saks Fifth Avenue.

Dre did not want to be in the ritzy department store. "Kareem, what the hell are we doing in here? This rich ass store. I am tryinna thug it: jeans, T-shirt, Tims. I got limited funds, and I'm not wasting it on these pricey ass clothes. Especially not to look like a fag."

Kareem silenced his older brother. "Listen, you're not in Philly. In life you're going to learn that the world is ninety percent image and ten percent wealth. You have us on radar with that damn white tee and jeans. This thing is, you could easily be wealthy enough to buy this property and all the clothes in it, but you're on their radar based on your image. You have a lot to learn, son. Take notes."

When they arrived in the men's department, Dre was bored. Rather than look around, he took a seat on one of the plush sofas, and forced Kareem to scoff. "Get up!" Kareem signaled for the Saks sales lady and asked her to give her brother a LA makeover.

Bianca looked Dre up and down with her sexy, beady eyes. In a sanguine tone, she responded, "I'm a wizard. I'll have him ready for Dublin's in no time."

Kareem reminded Dre, "Yes, you'll be bubblin' in Dublin's in no time."

Of all the times, Dre had heard *I Just Wanna Love U (Give it 2 Me)* off the Jay-Z The Dynasty album, he had never known that Dublin's was a LA club.

Bianca took Dre by the hand to the dressing area along with a slim velvet suit, a red hacking jacket and black pant. Dre wanted to resist, but Bianca had convinced him by the allure of the Gucci pieces. "Go ahead. Try it on. I'll be back with more pieces."

Kareem was in the Prada section going mad. He grabbed a few pieces for the night, but he would return for a few other things before he left LA.

Bianca returned to the dressing room and knocked on the door. In her French accent, she yelled quietly, "Come on out, Dre. It can't be that bad. Come out."

Dre came out with a grin on his face. "Dre Bezel the Great has gone Hollywood," he said conceitedly and popped his collar.

Kareem turned and saw that his brother looked like a million bucks. "Lose the arrogance, though, lil' nigga."

Dre looked at Bianca excitedly. "What else you got? I can get used to LA."

Kareem was unimpressed with his brother's new-found arrogance, and would pass along all of his elitist etiquette that he had learned in life. Kareem had no intention of changing Dre's mentality, but he would show him the ropes to garner what he desired in life, to be amongst the Talented Tenth. If Dre was as fast as Kareem at learning the ropes, he would climb the rope as quickly as his younger brother.

Dre chose three different ensembles, two watches, and three different types of footwear: Issey Miyake sneakers, Salvatore Ferragamo loafers, and D Squared boots. Kareem was flabbergasted.

When Bianca completed ringing up the purchases, it totaled $8,250.39. Dre complained, "Look, these things are nice, but..."

"Don't worry, I got this one," Kareem said and pulled out his cell phone. When the called party answered, he said, Hey, Madeline, this is David. I need for you to use the miscellaneous account to purchase some pieces for my L.A. Richard Tyler audition." After a brief pause, he said, "You're the damn publicist, and you work for me, so act like it!"

Publicist! Dre thought perplexed.

Kareem passed along the phone to Bianca who loved the way that Kareem treated the publicist. She hated people blocking other people's purchases, and ultimately her commission. At 10%, she stood to get $800 and some change from that purchase. She was seeing that sale through.

* * *

During the ride back to the hotel, Dre inquired what had happened at Saks. "Who the hell, or why do you have a damn publicist?"

"I don't."

"Then who the hell just paid for nine-grand in gear, nigga?"

Kareem's response was interrupted by his cell phone ringing. "Here she is now." After a brief conversation, Kareem gave the phone to Dre.

"Hello?" Dre spoke nervously.

"What's up, my nigga?" It was Marquis.

"Where's Madeline? The rich bitch."

"Right here, darling?" Marquis said, mimicking a woman's voice, startling Dre.

CHAPTER 36

*W*hen they arrived back to the hotel, Kareem decided that he would share some of his secrets with his older brother. Dre marched around the room in new gear like a kid at Christmas.

"Yo, if you can stop prancing around for a moment, I can bless you with something..."

"Hold up," Dre said, cutting him off. "I strut, not prance."

"Prancing, strutting. Tomaytoe. Tomahtoe. The key word here is listening. Get it. Got it. Good." After a pause, Kareem went on. "I already told you image trumps wealth, and by the way you're"—he cleared his throat—"strutting that is evident. Doing what I do is completely responsible for the total makeover of Jean-Mary's home. You complained that I was her favorite, so that was why I traded the Lexus for the Benz. No, I provided the cash for the down payment, and I pay the note. What I do is like taking candy from a baby, as you just saw at Saks. I use fake ID's—I call them faces—to buy shit with check books and credit cards that belong to someone else." Dre looked confused. Kareem continued, "Yeah your brother is up. Had you not been so wrapped in the drug game, which is bullshit by the way, you'd also be up. But make no mistake, you're going to be."

"So, how do I get down?"

"You don't. You fall back and chill. Let me do this." Kareem went to the bar and poured himself a screwdriver with extra orange juice.

"Kareem, I have the game sowed up with the Rican's. I can make a nice profit, if I am on my own."

"I can make that happen. Just sit back and chill for a minute, though. Just know that is a short ride. I have enough money to launch my entire line, and I am working on the advertising and manufacturing costs. You need to be securing the money to start that accounting/tax firm you wanted to do. Or have you lost that dream?"

"Naw. I still want to have a corporate chain of accounting firms and investment firms. What about McKenzey?"

"Fuck dat, clown! I already know that he is coming for us. I am a few steps ahead of him, though, and I am gonna do me. Period!"

"This is not chess." Dre reminded his little brother.

"Oh, it is my friend. And in the end, I'll be the one to check mate." Kareem let that sink in and then said, "Get dressed. We have some partying to do."

* * *

*A*t the bar, Dre ordered an Incredible Hulk—a mixed drink consisting of Hypnotiq and Hennessy, with a touch of vodka—and sipped the green libation with class. Dre titled his head back and swallowed the whole glass, and then ordered a vodka and orange juice.

Dre was engrossed in the Dublin and overall LA ambiance. It was much different than Philadelphia. He stood—to roam around--and Kareem grabbed him.

Kareem warned him, "You're a little tipsy. No cussin'. No blasphemous behavior. Be on your suave shit and the girls will flock."

"Now, you're telling me about women? What the fuck you know besides Toi, and she is a virgin, nigga!"

Kareem ignored that, because he had more notches on his belt than Dre could ever imagine. "Tell them you're from Philly and show off your six-pack. They'll want to fuck the drunken East Coast, nigga."

Kareem had more profitable things on his mind. His priority was himself, but Dre was equally important. His brother had been beguiled by the ghetto of Philadelphia. Now was the time to move on. Together the two of them could not be stopped. Kareem relaxed at the bar, sipping Seagram's gin. He decided to try the drink that Peety Pablo endorsed.

At two a.m., the brothers headed back to the hotel. Dre had scored a light skinned vixen named, Erin. Kareem thought that she looked better in the club. He hoped that Dre kept the room light dim like the club to augment her beauty.

* * *

Kareem lay in his hotel bed, ignoring Erin, whom played hard to get with Dre. Kareem could not believe the duckling played with his older brother's emotions. Kareem could not take the lies that she spat, so he exited stage left and landed in the tub. After relaxing in the bath, he lathered his body with the hotel lotion. He was restless. After a half-hour, he exited the bathroom, but tried to back up and not be noticed. Too bad, the bathroom light announced him like a Boeing jet landing on the White House lawn. Naked and tired of Erin's bullshit, Kareem walked out of the bathroom and hung his semi-hard dick in her face. He hated to step on his brother's toes, but he knew what she wanted. Why else would she be in their hotel room. *Non-committal sex*, he thought. The best kind.

She reached out and touched his hardness. He gripped himself and slapped her lips with his dick before he grabbed the back of her head and slipped himself into her mouth. Dre realized that his little brother, "the nerd," had stolen his bitch.

Erin wanted two dicks, so she motioned for Dre to move closer, and then reached out and pulled Dre's dick out his boxers.

Erin had a professional head game, too. An authentic Ph.D. in brain surgery. She had taken control of the situation, like a real woman should. She pushed Kareem back onto the bed and crawled over top of him and put him back into her mouth with her ass perched in the air. Dre seized the moment to put a leash on his dick, and then slipped deep into Erin's guts from the back. She let out a deep groan, and looked back smiling. She was a big girl. To prove it, Dre began to pound into her. He was sexually adroit and she was about to learn it.

After twenty minutes of exciting strokes, Dre sweated profusely. He dripped sweat on Erin's lower back as another ten minutes flew by. And then, he viciously attacked Erin's insides, she expected him to cum, and she pushed him out of her.

"Fuck me in the ass." She begged, and Dre obliged.

"Oh, I love that," she said, after Dre spit between her ass cheeks. When she was moist, he slid deep into her back door.

Dre controlled his rhythm, because he was already about to cum, but he didn't want to disappoint Erin, or look like a lame to his brother. After Dre began to cum, he pulled out of her and slipped the condom off. She let Kareem pop out of her mouth and she quickly turned around and deep throated Dre. She pulled on his shaft to milk him dry. "Get that pussy," she said to Kareem.

Kareem was impressed as Erin threw herself back on him. Again taking control, Erin pushed him back to the bed and she straddled over top of him and began to ride him.

Tough!

Express!

Leisurely!

Profound!

Crush!

Recoil!

Dre was in the background watching Kareem go to work. He had watched Saved by the Bell's Screech, grow up before his eyes. Kareem had slapped her ass cheeks and helped her bounce on him. He gripped up her waist and forced her to slam hard against his pelvis. She loved every moment, and let him know, by continually telling him to, "Beat that pussy up, nigga. Kill that shit."

"You like this Philly dick, don't you?" Kareem boasted, right before he came. He pulled out of her, and said, "Let me bust all over your face".

She grinned. "Bust all of over this face," she said, and lapped up every drop that escaped his dick.

Without a second thought, Erin gathered her things, dressed and left the hotel room. When the door closed behind her both brothers looked at each other and busted out in laughter. The joke was on Erin.

CHAPTER 37

*T*he following day, Kareem was alarmed to hear a knock on the hotel door. He opened it and found, Toi and Marquis. Toi jumped into Kareem's arms, while he avoided face-to-face contact. He had not brushed his teeth and did not want her to feel the heat of his morning breath. He put her down and disappeared into the bathroom.

Restlessly, Kareem emerged from the bathroom and got back under the covers. Toi sat next to him and rested her head on his shoulders.

Marquis sat at the desk and flipped through the hotel guide, as Kareem told him and Toi about the police station drama. He strategically left out the private investigator portion of the story. He didn't want to alarm Toi into thinking that he would have an investigator follow her. Toi was fascinated, but she was eager to hit the luxurious streets of Hollywood. She sat there done from head to toe, ready for Sunset Boulevard.

Kareem picked up the phone and called, Bianca. Marquis went through his luggage and pulled out a handful of fresh, stolen credit card numbers with all of the customers information included.

With the clothes on the way, Kareem asked Dre and Marquis, "What are ya'll doing today? There's no way that we are going to flank Toi like body guards."

Toi gave Kareem an encouraging smile, before she said, "That may not be a bad idea, though. Give LA the idea that I am a celebrity."

Marquis answered, "We don't need ya'll. I got this. Dre, pack what you have, I'mma get you your own room, and then we outta here."

Marquis took Dre to the front desk and got them both their own hotel rooms on the same floor as Kareem's. He had left Kareem with a folder full of all the essentials, he needed to do his business in Los Angeles.

* * *

*A*t two-thirty, Kareem and Toi exited the staircase on the main level of the Grafton and had all eyes on them. Toi wore the sexy Mandarin-like scent of Dior Bronze Sweet Sun fragrance by Christian Dior. Kareem had spritzed on a soft musk scent of Yves St. Laurent Rive Gauche Pour Hommes, a complimentary gift from Bianca. Bianca had also sent Kareem a white with yellow pin stripe technical mesh blazer, and pant, both, Burberry Prosum. His attire complimented Toi's yellow strapless number by Tom Ford for Gucci. They were an up-and-coming Will and Jada entering the stretch limo to tour the celebrity homes of Hollywood.

Toi was excited to see where the celebrities laid their heads during their down time. Kareem was equally excited, but his excitement was smooth and restrained. They took photos of the experience.

Kareem eventually looked deep into her eyes and romantically put his arm around her shoulders. "Make no mistake. One day…We will live like this, fo' sho'."

Toi rested her head on his shoulder and trusted his every word.

* * *

Dre and Marquis were on a more mischievous mission. They had attacked Rodeo Drive and the Beverly Center with stolen credit cards. Dre had more bags in his hands than a street bum. He hadn't stopped shopping until he couldn't carry another bag.

At every boutique they went into, Dre looked in amazement, and asked each clerk for the hottest clubs and underground nightspots in the city.

Along with the shopping, Marquis had the duty to further bring Dre into the twenty-first century. Kareem had focused on image. Now, Marquis set out to focus on wealth. Marquis emphasized the importance of a plentiful financial security blanket. He noted the worth of stacking cash, while pursuing a dream career to get out of any illegal activity. "Shoot to be an entrepreneur in the field that you love most, so that you'll live a rewarding life doing what you're loyal too," was the words that most inspired Dre.

Dre was forced to see that there was something outside the ghetto, and rich, white people were not the only ones privy to it.

CHAPTER 38

*T*oi and Kareem had requested that the limo driver take them to the most luxurious home décor stores in LA. When they entered the first showroom, Kareem was in heaven on Earth. He and his wife-to-be shopped to furnish their first home together. The moment was special and would be cherished for a lifetime.

With his good checkbook in hand, Kareem settled on a chocolate crocodile sofa and loveseat, with over-sized removable arms. It was worth $17,000. He had the interior designer ring up a brown tripod style lamp with a cream lamp shade that was covered in a world map.

Kareem had the things shipped to a vacant apartment in Marquis' New York building. The landlord had trusted Marquis to show off the apartment to potential renters, but he only showed the apartment to Fed-Ex drivers and loose women. Kareem would have the furniture shipped to his home, as soon as it arrived. Toi and Kareem discussed the color scheme that they wanted throughout the loft and decided on chocolate and cream to compliment the hardwood floor and cream marble abacus.

Out of curiosity, Toi asked, "How are we paying for this spree?"

Kareem paused and grinned devilishly inside. *We're not*, he thought as he prepared his lie. He hated to lie to her, but he was aware that men showed signs of weakness when they brought their villainous-street behavior home. He told her, "My dad left over...well the amount is not important...but the money was for my college fund. As you know I had a full scholarship, so I am using that money to buy whatever you and I want."

"What ever I want?" she asked and snuggled up to him. She kissed his ear lobe and whispered into his ear, "Are you sure?"

He shifted his head and let his lips touch hers. "You can have anything," he told her, before he kissed her salaciously.

When he released her, she tapped on the limo driver's window. "Take us to Burberry."

* * *

*S*everal hours later, at six-thirty Kareem and Toi returned to the hotel room for a candle lit dinner. They had the limo driver stop them at a movie shop and they bought *Love Don't Cost a Thing* and *You Got Served*.

They ate dinner and reflected on their relationship, and where they saw themselves in the years to come. They set goals and time tables to complete them. That was their favorite pass time.

Toi had become tired and preferred to stay in and not go out to any clubs. Kareem was fine with that, because he did not want to run into Erin, or any other chicks that he flirted with the night before.

After getting comfortable, they shared ice cream, which they fed each other. Toi had her head rested on his chest, dressed in a Fredericks of Hollywood nightie. They watched a movie and cuddled.

Midway through the movie, Kareem caressed Toi softly. She emoted, relishing the moment. She looked up into his eyes and a look of passion and emotion forced her to move up to kiss his lips.

Softly.

Her kissed progressed and became forceful and aggressive. He perceived, her kisses indicated how she wanted to be made love to. She was ready to lose her virginity, right there in LA. Kareem thought strange things only happened in Vegas. He turned off the TV and turned on The Beat, the urban station. Slow jams played, mellowing the mood another notch.

On his way back to the bed, Kareem lost his boxers along the way. Back on the bed, he pulled Toi's nightie over her head. He removed her bra and then planted soft kisses upon her breasts. Just as anxious, Toi removed her panties and climbed on top of Kareem. The two kissed intensely. He wanted to slide his pistol up into her badly, but he did not want to appear fiendish, or rush her. This was her special moment.

Exhibiting her lust, she grabbed his manhood and attempted to sit down on it. He watched the pain shoot across her face. Her face was twisted with horror, and her body shivered. She released an anguished groan, sprang to her feet, and threw herself on the bed. He grabbed her tightly. Planted kisses down her midsection until he reached her wet spot. He kissed it a few times and led himself to believe that, he kissed it to make it feel better. For the moment, because he was finishing the job. He wanted things to be just right for her first time. After, he had given her the first oral orgasm of her life. She pulled his head up, and whispered, "Fuck me, Reem."

He wrapped her legs around his waist, and told her to entwine her feet together and rest them on his back. "I'mma put the head in and then you use your feet to pull me in deeper. As much as you want."

She shook her head up and down, as she stared at him. When he entered her, she sighed, but did not make an attempt to pull him in deeper. He took it upon himself and slowly entered deeper and deeper into her, not pulling out.

When his waist was nearly rested against hers, she told him to, "Stop." Her arms wrapped tight around his back, and she told him, "It hurts so badly, Reem, but it feels good, too. And I want to do it."

He pulled out and told her, "You have to relax baby. You're going to open up. This pain is going to go away. I promise." *I'm tryinna beat this thing up. You are long the fuck over due.*

She gained her composure and decided that she wanted to make her man happy. She grabbed his dick and felt it. Ran her hand across the length, and told herself, I can take all this. She gained control, and garnered courage to guide him into her. She couldn't believe how wet that she was. She knew what it felt like moments earlier when he had made her orgasm and she wanted to please him the same way.

R. Kelly's *The Greatest Sex* blasted through the radio and Kareem whispered the lyrics into her ear. Affectionately, she grabbed his ass and slowly pulled him further into her.

She let out a subtle moan. And then another. Biting on his neck, lightly. She was determined to give him something to remember.

She convinced herself that the difficult part was over and gained the nerve to endure the pleasurable pain. She boldly winded her hips slowly to meet his grinding thrusts. She continued to grind after he remained still to let her get it all by herself. "That's all you, Toi," he said, looking deeply into her eyes, and sexually bit his bottom lip.

She appeared to be comfortable, so he slowly pulled out of her—up to the head—and then plunged his entire piece into her. He was mesmerized by how deep and wet that she was. He entered her deeper and harder. He felt his dick head tap on her deepest wall. Her cherry, he thought. Toi was no longer a virgin, after Kareem made his way through that.

Forty-five minutes worth of intimate strokes later, Toi pumped harder and pulled Kareem deeper into her. He felt her body shiver, and knew that she had climaxed a second time. He rushed and plowed into her and they came together.

PART THREE

AUGUST 2005
(Two Summers Later)

CHAPTER 39

*T*oi sat at a cozy table for two at Justin's, P. Diddy's upscale restaurant in New York City. Kareem had her meet him there for their weekly Wednesday "Hump Day" lunch date. After she waited twenty minutes, Toi felt agitated and lost her urge to be around Kareem. Although, she worked at a high-end home décor retailer, she relentlessly complained about Kareem's work habits. She worked on the debut interior design line, but had doubts that she would be in Kareem's life to debut it with his clothing line.

Another ten minutes rolled by and Toi snatched her cell phone off the table to call her mother.

"Toi, baby, what's wrong," her mother asked, having read her daughter's mood.

"I'm stressed."

"Stressed from what, Latoya?"

"Mom, I do not know exactly. Kareem!"

"Please do not tell me Kareem's busy schedule is the problem, again. Baby, he loves you, and you have not given me reason to think otherwise. You better grow up before you loose a good man. There ain't many."

"Excuse me! A good man for whom, mom? You or I? I have to live with robot man. Not you."

"He's a robot because he is a hard worker. You silly little girl. I have raised you better. He is making a way for you two to live forever. Don't you dare blow it."

"Blow it? Listen, I better talk to you later." Toi stared up at the ceiling, desperately attempting to prevent the tears from falling.

Moments later a tall, brown-skinned man approached her. She gathered herself when the man helped himself to a seat at her table.

The strange man said to her, "Excuse me, beautiful, but why the long face?"

"Can you excuse yourself? My boyfriend will be here any minute now." She was polite, but wanted to get to the point.

"Damn, do not be so mean. Is he the problem?"

"Gee, you're right," she said sarcastically. "So, like him, and other men, you would never understand."

"I would over-stand, try me. I am a good listener." He did not want to lose the opportunity to talk to her.

"You're a stranger and I seriously doubt that you can effectively advise me. Besides you do not even know me."

"Come on. Psych's do it every day."

"Yeah, they take at least a half hour to hear a client's past, prior to helping them. My boyfriend, as I said, should be here any minute now, so we hardly have time for that."

"I think that he's the problem. Stood you up, huh? Probably the second time, too. You have been here forty-five minutes alone."

"We will be fine. Just need to iron some things out."

"You should iron him right out your life. But good luck though. Retouch your lipstick, sexy."

Toi pulled out her lipstick and hit her lips. Before she could put it into her purse, he lightly grabbed her hand and took her lipstick from her. He then used it to write his number and name on a napkin.

"Call me, if you ever want to talk over lunch. I promise not to be late. Or stand you up, like you're boyfriend." He simply left the table, without allowing her to respond.

"Uh, Shimir," she called out, having learned his name from the napkin. "I doubt that I ever call you."

"Your loss," he said, and continued away from the table. He was the prize.

Toi slipped the number into her pocket as Kareem looked at her. She had no idea that he was in disbelief. He stood at the host station and watched her interaction with Shimir. He calmed down. Maybe she knew him.

Kareem approached her and she did not stand to hug him as usual. He became further pissed.

"Toi, I was trapped in a crazy traffic jam and New York's finest stopped me, for using my cell phone without an ear-piece. I was tryinna call you."

Toi looked at him, as if she didn't give a damn. Kareem knew how to get words out of her, though.

"You were not silent when that pariah was all up in your face." Kareem was mad, and she knew it.

She was equally mad, but she was ready to talk, since he attacked her. "He's an after thought. Don't go there."

"Do you have his number?"

"No, boy—"

"Man!" Kareem had to correct her. He had long ago stopped being a boy. "So, you knew that clown?"

"Look, it doesn't matter. What, I can't have a conversation with a damn man? I did not come here to be harassed by your dumb ass." She stood and headed to the exit. "Urghh, you urk the shit out of me."

Kareem sat there stunned. He watched her walk out the door. Knowing, he could not let her leave without chasing her, he pounded his hand on the table. Other patrons looked. He went into his wallet and threw $50 on the table and told the maitre d', "Excuse me, this will never happen again. Here is my card. Contact me if there are any charges that need to be settled." The maitre d' smiled as Kareem ran after Toi.

Kareem had graduated from Columbia U last summer, and he put in four days a week at *GQ*, which was largely responsible for helping him launch his line. His *GQ* contacts enabled him to schmooze with manufacturers and distributors who wanted to mass produce his line. He planned to use them, but he had contingency plans, too. To cut the first-year over head, he had been searching for a foreign warehouse to manufacture his line. Now, he had to chase after his woman. Had he not, she would have complained that he did not chase her because, he did not love her. *What the fuck, I don't have time for this bullshit.*

CHAPTER 40

*U*nder the restaurant canopy, he looked both ways like a second grader crossing the street alone. He spotted her red blouse, and then dashed behind her.

He caught up to her, but she continued walking. "Toi, please stop walking." He knew that she was wrong, but he remained in control. The man of the house. He was pissed that she kept walking, and common sense compelled him not to choke her. "Toi!" He yelled. He gave himself a second to calm down and then he spoke in a refrained tone. "I cannot believe that you would walk out on me in the middle of a packed restaurant. You whine about the dumbest things, and I do not deserve this bullshit! I refuse to fail, so I work hard. Better yet, I can't fail. I've made it too far and sacrificed too much. You know that. In a year or two, an antic like that would make it out of the mouths of bitches like, Wendy Williams. I ain't going for this drama, Latoya." He stopped talking because, she had not paid him any attention.

"All you worry about is your image. What about me? Fuck you and your image, nigga."

Kareem could not believe that she had flagged a taxi and hopped in. He stood in front of the taxi, preventing it from pulling off. "Toi don't leave me here, or you better have this mutha fucka take you to Amtrak, to get you on a one way ride to your mom's."

She ignored him He moved out the way, and she rolled away.

Kareem trekked to his car and sat in it. He loosened his tie and tossed it in the back seat. He thought of their few arguments. They were mild and he usually controlled how they elevated. He was mature, and he found it beneath him to argue with a woman. He had too much confidence. A lot of swagger.

He went into his trunk and put in the R. Kelly *Chocolate Factory* CD. Back in the car, he played track three: *I Will Never Leave.*

Kareem's cell phone rang, and he ignored it. He was then chirped.

"Kareem answer your phone." It was Rhonda, his cousin, best friend, and confidante."

He picked up his phone on the second ring when she called back. "Cousin, what's happening?"

"Nothing, chillen. Just calling to let you know that I opened three corporate casino accounts."

"That's good, baby girl. Let me get at you later."

After ten minutes of sulking, rather than cry his anger and misunderstanding out, Kareem bottled it up and drove to the Royal Theater to see *"A Raisin in the Sun."*

CHAPTER 41

After the play, Kareem had his Play Bill signed by Phylicia Rashad. He drove up Madison Avenue to his loft, as he gathered his mettle to face Toi. He knew that he had to be canny with his words to her. This was, of course, if she was home. One thing was for sure: Kareem had not been the staunchest man, but his infidelity was clandestine.

He parked, and entered the lobby of his building. He nodded to the doorman and checked his mailbox. It was full. Not the norm. Was Toi home? This entire conundrum arose because he was a hard worker. *This is bullshit*, he thought, as he rode the elevator to his floor. *I don't need this and I don't deserve it.*

He opened his loft door, and found music playing. She was home, but why the *Waiting to Exhale* soundtrack? *Is it that deep*?

With no sight of her, he went to the bedroom. There she lied on the bed flipping through an Essence magazine, singing along with the soundtrack. He sat his briefcase on the floor, hung up his blazer, and sat on his side of the bed. He searched for the words to say to her.

He undressed, put on his robe, and then headed to the shower. Toi stalked behind him. He stopped abruptly, knowing that she was in pursuit, and she bumped into him. Now she blushed, after she had been making weird faces behind his back. She walked past him without words. Kareem grabbed her.

"What the fuck is?" He stopped talking to refrain from using the epithet. "What is the problem, Toi?" He was serious and she did not see any of his usual charm.

"You stopped, so I bumped into you," she said, dumbfounded. "Sorry." And she had an attitude.

"Toi, Toi, Toi." He let out a deep breath and shook his head in obvious disgust. "You know that I am not talking about you slamming into me, Latoya. You're becoming more and more irrational. I thought your feelings of neglect would be short, and that we were past that? I must have been wrong."

Toi, determined to be obstinate, stared at him blinking her eyes uncontrollably to avoid tears. After no words and reflecting on her mother's words, she fell back into the wall. Kareem watched her and became annoyed; he never thought that she would ignore him.

She slid down the wall, and a tsunami of tears followed. "I'm sorry. So, sorry, Kareem," Toi proclaimed, and broke down. On the floor, face in her palms, resting on her knees, she sobbed.

Her sudden emotional change startled Kareem. He was confused. He knew that he worked hard, but she also had some guy's number in her pants pocket. He sat next to her, pulled her close to him and placed her head on his shoulder.

"Don't cry, baby. Please don't cry." He rocked side to side and patted her like a tyke.

Moments later, she regained her composure and her outburst reduced to sniffing. She sat up and Kareem kneeled in front of her, and cleared her tears with his finger tips. He kissed her closed eyes, and then went down her cheeks, slipping his tongue into her mouth. He kissed her and they stood up slowly.

She pulled away from him, "Kareem, I am so, sorr…"

He pressed his lips to hers and squelched her. "Pretty, I work hard all for you. *GQ*, Chase, the gym, and the clothing line—all for you. You have nothing to worry about. I have a lifetime of fidelity just for a special lady. You! No need to explain your behavior. No need to apologize, just do not let this happen again." His words were soft, albeit stern and she took him as meaning every syllable.

He picked her up and carried her up to the loft. She was about to be erotically punished. And she deserved it for being a bad girl.

CHAPTER 42

Dre lived in New York, too, and had been a model citizen of the Big Apple, and loving father and fiancé. He purchased a four-bedroom in the Bronx and moved Tasha and Amare there. Tasha was a stay at home mom, while he attended New York University's accounting certificate program. He also had transferred to a New York post office. Kareem received most of his credit cards from this office, where Dre stole them by the dozens. He also stole checks, Social Security cards, and bank statements.

When Dre arrived to his duplex, around ten p.m., all he wanted was dinner and some love. Wednesday's were hardest for him, because after work, he had to attend classes. When he walked into the door, he was greeted by Amare, who climbed slowly off the sofa and walked to Dre's feet to be picked up. He yelled, "Honey, I'm home," with a big grin on his face.

Tasha walked out the kitchen and responded, "That was so Cliff Huxtable."

"So, I guess that makes you, Claire?"

"And they say you can take the boy out the ghetto, but not the ghetto out the boy."

Dre raised his latest accounting test in the air with one arm, and held Amare with the other. "B-minus. Not an A, but better than the last C."

Tasha hugged him, completing the family hug and congratulated him.

"Where's the food at? A nigga is starving."

Tasha proceeded to the kitchen. "Right this way, sir," she said, smiling. She used an English accent, extending her arm toward the kitchen. Life was grand.

She placed a hot meal in front of him and he ate a baked potato with his hands, Tasha shook her head. "I guess, I spoke to soon. There is that ghetto-ness."

"Never leave home without it."

They both smiled, and he swallowed his meal like a starving American hostage in Iraq. When he was done, he tossed his dish into the washer, as Tasha cleaned the pots. He took them from her, grabbed a kitchen towel, and then dried her hands.

"Enough of that Florence shit. Let's put..." Dre nodded his head toward Amare, who beat the refrigerator with a truck. "To bed so, you know, we can..." Dre winked his eye and tugged on his dick.

Tasha spied the erection unfolding like a movie plot in front of Dre's pants, and eagerly snatched up Amare and put him to bed.

* * *

*A*gent Lucas McKenzey was dog tired. He looked like a dog, with his tongue hung out, thirsty from trying to nail both Bezel brothers. He traveled to New York and sat with his gun trained on them from inside his car. He vowed to get even, but killing them was too easy. He wanted to be sure there was no inheritance. Besides, he was out to humiliate.

He sat around for two years and allowed things to die down. He had not rested knowing Dre and an accomplice got away with killing Snobli. His narcissistic mental state, forced him to love watching the blood splatter from Snobli's brain at the crime scene. *Still, the monkey's had to be punished for their crimes.*

So, there was McKenzey taking matters into his own hands. He was especially mad that he had to deal with a shortage of funds, as BG was no longer bringing in the bacon.

The lights turned off in Dre's home, as McKenzey looked on. *I can get that pussy, now.* He was enraged and eager to get revenge. *No, I have to wait. They're laughing now, but I will get the last laugh.*

CHAPTER 43

Dre arrived at the post office at 33rd Street and 8th Avenue and wondered, why he continued a life of boredom. He envisioned being part of a more dangerous profession. Kareem had supplied everything that he needed with credit cards, so he did not complain about saving his cash. But Dre wanted to be free to get involved with handling his business in the Philadelphia drug game. Chino had things under control and the two were in constant contact. But Dre was a born hustler, and the 9-5 thing was becoming increasingly harder to deal with.

With Kareem's help, Chino and Dre had been able to cop a wide range of drugs and a distinct clientele of the baller persuasion, and Dre wanted to be hands on. Right in the mix.

* * *

Kareem sat at his Chase desk with a seemingly wealthy couple: The Flemings. According to their account summary, they had been customers for ten years. They started with a $1,200 deposit from an income tax return. They now had an aggregate $680,271.04 balance among three accounts. They came into the branch to withdraw $250,000 in cash. Kareem was handed their New York driver license, several credit cards, and withdrawal slip signatures that matched those that the bank had on file.

Mr. Fleming was a light hued man and sported a salt-and-pepper beard with more salt than pepper. He had a noticeable mole on his left cheek along side deep-set dimples. He was not obese, but fairly overweight. Mrs. Fleming, a petite 45-year-old, looked much younger than her husband. Her face sported a beauty mark above her silicone-pumped cheeks. She was perfectly painted to hide her true age.

The Flemings expressed their desire to vacation in Mexico, as well as, buy a summer home there while on vacation. Despite their convincing alibi for the cash, Kareem called Ms. Warren, the bank assistant manager, to approve the transaction. He did not want to relinquish that much cash without a second set of eyes.

Ms. Warren looked annoyed at their identification, credit cards, and signatures. She then took the materials over to her desk and pulled up their account on her computer. The Flemings had made a $3,000 withdrawal the day before at a teller's window. She called Mr. Fleming's job and found, he was on a vacation for two weeks.

She returned to Kareem's desk and asked Mr. Fleming the date and amount of the last withdrawal on the account. She needed to be further convinced.

With one eyebrow raised, Mrs. Fleming decided to answer. "Yesterday. For $3,000. To purchase a vacation package. Is there anything else, we have a plane to catch?"

Kareem spun around from his computer and removed his gold horn-rimmed Cartier glasses. "Mrs. Fleming we are trying to protect you and your money. We are sorry for any inconvenience, but we have to take these precautions with all of the theft and identity stealing going on in the world." He gave her a curt smile and hoped that she was satisfied.

"Everything is fine," Ms. Warren said. "Mr. Bezel, follow me." To the Flemings, she said, "We will be back with your cash."

CHAPTER 44

Rhonda shuddered as she awaited Kareem's return. Marquis had sweaty palms and was slightly lethargic. They both needed to calm down. Sweating would not be good for their costumes. Marquis had borrowed the extra thirty pounds, beard, and make up to pull off the heist from his theater program at NYU. Marquis and Rhonda morphed into the Flemings for hours, but they had a $250,000 reward for the work.

When Kareem knocked on the room door on the 10th floor of the Helmsley Park Lane Hotel, Rhonda and Marquis was relieved. Rhonda hugged him and Kareem went to the window and looked out over Central Park. It was a lovely command center to coordinate how the money would be broken down.

Marquis, the marketing and promotions director of Kareem's company had graduated from NYU and now studied Fashion Marketing at the Fashion Institute of Technology. He had momentarily given up his acting career, well, in the traditional sense. He had thought about settling down with a woman, having been jealous of Kareem's and Dre's love affairs. Meanwhile, he was bogged down looking for the best location for Kareem to open a flagship store in New York. He also looked for the perfect venue to debut the fashion line. Marquis poured glasses of champagne and tapped his glass with a fork. "To a long and prosperous life," he said, toasting the amazing theft.

"You two were great. Just like a real husband and wife. I saw Rhonda about to attack you for snatching that duffle bag full of money."

"I missed the *no* nod," Rhonda said, a little disappointed that she had missed Kareem's cue at the bank.

"Don't worry, you were good for your first time," Kareem said, and gave her an encouraging hug. To Marquis, he said, "How much did Men's Vogue say a full page ad was?"

"$90,000." Marquis said after consulting his notes.

"They have to be kidding," Rhonda said. Her eyes bulging and mouth open at the amount.

"Fine. Reserve six pages tomorrow. What do the contractors need?"

"They're waiting to quote until they have the square footage. Everything hinges on the size of the property."

"Let's have that location list narrowed by Friday, so that we can make a selection and get production under way."

"Hello, I'm still here," Rhonda said, rolling her eyes.

"Sorry, Rhonda. $25,000 should send you on your merry little way," Kareem said, smiling. Usually they split the profits, but the team was on a mission. Avariciousness could not be apart of the equation.

"That money is fine, but I want to be apart of the company," Rhonda said.

"No problem. I need an advertising director."

"Looks like you have one," she said.

CHAPTER 45

On Saturday, Kareem, Dre and Marquis sat at Planet Hollywood, just off Fifth Avenue. They watched a large wall-mounted plasma TV, waiting for the horse race at the Belmont Stakes to commence. Marquis had wanted to head to Long Island to watch the race, however the trio had to do a job the next day.

"Gentleman, are we ready to order?" the waiter asked.

Marquis sent the waiter to get three fruit punches. He needed the brothers sober. "What's the deal with you?" He asked Kareem. "You look fucked up."

"To cut to the chase, last week I watched Toi slip some ugly nigga's number in her pocket."

"You didn't fuck her up?" Dre asked, quickly. "You better than me, 'cause, I'd be on Rikers looking forward to death row."

"Where was she at?" Marquis asked, half-heartedly believing his ears.

"Relishing a wasted puffy shrimp appetizer, and white wine at Justin's," Kareem explained, and then gave them the full 411.

"Damn. What the hell was she thinking?" Dre asked as he patted his brother's shoulder.

Marquis then said, "Doesn't she realize how good you are to her. Not only financially, but mentally. I cannot believe that she was crazy enough to be cozened."

"Cozened! What the fuck is cozened?" Dre asked. "Ebonics, mutha fuckas."

"If you can't keep up, stay out of the conversation."

Dre ignored Marquis. "I'm not sugar coating this. You're a damn fool. When Tasha cheated on me, Jean-Mary warned us both to be aware of our girlfriends. She told us to play the field, not to get caught up with one bitch at our young ages. Now look at you, the smart one."

The waiter fluttered to the table and accidentally bumped into it. He placed flutes in front of them, filled with fruit punch. That gave Kareem a chance to gather a response and invite them to Atlantic City, New Jersey.

CHAPTER 46

In the sticky heat of August, Kareem seized the moment to invite Dre and Marquis on a trip to Atlantic City. During the drive, the three of them talked about the clothing line. Finally, Kareem turned off the music and made an announcement.

"Yo! That was D-Block, fool," Dre shouted from the back seat.

"Calm down. I need both of your attention."

"Here we go," Marquis said.

"Look in my briefcase. There's a manila envelope. Pull it out and take the folder that is yours, and give the other one to Marquis."

"What the fuck is my face doing on this ID?" Dre asked. He was puzzled.

Kareem smiled. "That's the new you. For the stay at the AC hotel at least." When that sank in without any questions, Kareem said, "Study the profile. Once at the casino, you will use all that you have to be convincing enough to clear the accounts of its cash and at least double it gambling."

"What the hell am I supposed to do with this?" Dre asked, having paid Kareem's instructions no attention. He was still puzzled.

Marquis understood perfectly.

The troika pulled up to the Trump Taj Mahal and was ready to rock. Even though Dre's stomach churned, he planned to pull off the job. They entered the lobby, side-by-side, in their power suits. All eyes watched them. They strutted to the music made by the slot machines and gamblers cheering. What a grand beat.

Kareem had his left hand in his pocket, just far enough for the coiled Philippe Cherriol watch to show. Dre's ears glistened with the four-karat Harry Winston studs in his ear lobes. The yellow diamonds shone like a block of frozen lemonade. Marquis had on a Barry Keiselstein-Cord belt with a gaudy crocodile buckle, which was brilliant against his all black attire. The three amigos, led by the fraud baron, Kareem, checked into their suites and then headed to the casino. Each of them took $20,000 in chips against their room accounts and hit the casino, prepared to triple the $20,000.

* * *

*T*oi laid across the king-sized bed with her feet propped up on the leather footboard. She stared around, listening to Sade. Bored, she decided to call Tasha, who was busy chasing after the screaming Amare.

"Dre needs to have his ass here," Tasha said, provoking Toi's anger that both brothers had left them alone.

"Experiencing loneliness, huh? And I thought that it was only me?"

"I understand my man's mission, Toi. I just need to deal with it for now."

Is this bitch crazy? Toi thought. "Better you than me."

"Maybe I should have a hot...no...fervent, love affair," Tasha joked.

Toi had taken that into consideration. *You have no fuckin' idea.*

"You sound foolish," Toi said, lying. That was a good idea to her at that moment. She heard Amare screaming and decided that she had better let Tasha go.

Fed up with her imaginary neglect, she pulled out her cell phone and pushed *SEND* when she reached an entry in her phone book for Samira.

"Hi, may I speak to Shimir?" He acknowledged that it was him, and she went on. "You may not remember me, but I'm the girl that you met at Justine's a few weeks ago."

"Oh, I remember you. What, Don Juan dumped you?"

"No. He's away on business. Once again, leaving me alone." She had a hint of anger in her voice. "And he's no, Don Juan."

"Sounds like he's gambling with his relationship. So, is that the reason you called me. Am I the rebound? To be used for sympathy sex, I hope."

"No...and no! To be honest, I do not know why I called. I guess I just needed to talk to a man."

"You have one." He was sarcastic. *Talk!* He had no desire to converse. He was more in the mood for a good bedroom assault.

"You have a real potty-mouth, sir." She smiled.

"No profanity, sis. That's not ladylike." He joked. "So, since he's away, what do you say to me treating you to dinner and a movie?"

* * *

After hours of gambling, something came over Kareem.

Toi!

In an instant their life together flashed before him. Kareem sat at a poker table daydreaming when the house intruded.

"Mr. Gem, your bet," the woman said, calling him by his moniker, Mr. Gem.

"Sorry." Kareem looked around the table to find everyone had folded except a vivacious woman and him.

The cards shown for the table were a ten of hearts, a jack of hearts and an ace of clubs. Kareem had in the hole the ace and queen of hearts. The woman bet $5,000. Kareem called. He chased that royal flush; after all, he was not playing with his money. The house flipped the next card. The woman immediately cheered with her girlfriends. Kareem was not the least bit pressed when the woman bet $20,000. He saw her bet and raised her $5,000, to which she happily re-raised him another $20,000.

"You silly man. A nice looking man, but silly," the woman said, as the dealer flipped the river card.

An ace of diamonds. The woman cheered and went all in. Kareem called her and the woman flipped over a full house: aces over jacks.

"Laugh now," Kareem said, and flipped over that royal. He collected his chips and then headed to his room.

On the way there, he met his homeys at the casino bar, and informed them that he was going for a massage. He reminded them to meet him in the lobby of the hotel by 6:15 a.m. to get to the Philadelphia International Airport by 7:30.

* * *

Toi and Shimir exited the elegantly decorated Junior's Restaurant and Bakery after dinner. Toi was impressed with the legendary cheesecake, and felt good being out on a regular date.

"I really couldn't believe Bucktown, Brooklyn, had such a delicious cheesecake," Toi said, as they walked to Hoyt and Schermerhorn Streets toward the A and C trains.

"It's crazy that you've never been there. You being a five-star chick and all."

"I am a classy bitch. Thank you so much, for noticing."

"I guess it must be nice to be in a relationship with a high-class toy?"

"No, he's my boyfriend and far from a toy."

"If you're so proud, why are you walking from Junior's with me, after dinner and a movie? And only God knows where lover boy is."

"I don't know," she said, and paused. She gathered herself and said, "He's into some shit and I fear that he may get locked up, but I lie to him to make him think that his hectic schedule is my problem. If he don't get locked up, it may be worse."

"What is he a man-whore, 'cause I know he ain't a dope boy. None of that sort of shit."

Toi chuckled. "You have such a sense of humor."

"Word? He's probably rich." He could use the third party information. "That brings me to my original question. Why are you out with me? He's a prissy, soon-to-be-millionaire."

"You seem to think that you have him all figured out. He's far from prissy. More like well appointed."

"You seem to be doing nothing but complimenting him, so I do not see what seems to be the problem with him that has you in Brooklyn with me. Nevertheless, I enjoyed my night with you. *Baaadassss!* was a good movie pick, too." He stopped, then added, "So, I guess I can call you later, friend?" he asked, glad that she had distanced herself; otherwise, he'd be kissing her good night.

"No, I'll call you. He'll be home tonight."

"Okay, Get back to your prissy man in Manhanttenville safely."

They both chuckled and smiled at each other, as she disappeared underground into the subway.

CHAPTER 47

*B*right and early, Kareem, Dre and Marquis jumped into the back of a limo, and took another step closer to their dreams. An hour later, they boarded an American Airlines flight headed to Miami. After an hour layover, they boarded another flight to Medellin, Colombia, headed for the Medellin Jose Maria Cordova International Airport. After they cleared customs, they were greeted by a sedan driven by the workers of Salazar Ramirez. They drove for what seemed like hours, and watched the lively city civilization morph into jungle and then mountains.

Salazar's castle-like home looked like it dated to the Renaissance era and was located up in the hills. They parked along the side of a Benz and a Hummer, and Salazar met them in a rotund driveway. The man stood at five-feet-four-inches, with thinned hair tied into a ponytail. He had a Mexican mustache and a five o'clock shadow.

Three meagerly dressed young women groped the American's for weapons. Upon inspections, Salazar shook all of their hands. "Good to finally meet you," he said to Kareem in a high-pitched voice as he nearly crushed Kareem's hand with his large paw.

Dre said, "This is my team, Prodigy and Mar-Mar," as Salazar escorted them to his dining room.

A long cherry wood table filled the room from end to end, along with paintings on the walls of iconic Colombians. The ceiling was painted to resemble a cloudy sky. Two bonny women pulled out their chairs. "Would you like a drink," one of them asked.

"Naw, we straight." Dre answered for everyone.

"Well, then, let's get down to business." Salazar sat back in his large chair and rested his hands on his potbelly. He snapped his fingers and had a woman place a cigar in his mouth. After she lit it, he asked, "You three smoke?"

None of them did, but they elected to puff on the luxuriant cigar filled with the purest weed.

Dre sat up, adjusted his shirt collar and recited what he wanted. "I am interested in purchasing large quantities of cocaine and heroine. I have access to cash and valid credit cards to satisfy the debt."

Salazar moved in his seat, plucked his ashes into an ashtray held next to him by one of his woman, and asked, "What purpose would I need valid credit cards for?"

Kareem took over. "We thought it would be appropriate if we could give you payment in cash, and partial credit cards. We could pay 100-percent extra on the credit card end. I'm employed with the second largest bank in the states. Not only can I produce the cards, but I can monitor them, and I have the capability to launder funds."

Salazar tented his hands, leaned his elbows on the table, and responded, "Let's see here. If I agreed to this, how do you gentleman propose getting the product pass Homeland?"

"That's an easy one to answer." Marquis said. "Upon finalizing a deal with you, we are headed to purchase a warehouse." He gestured toward Kareem, and continued. "This guy here plans to have clothing for his fashion line manufactured here in Colombia. We intend to get the clothes shipped to America, and have the drugs secured in the clothing linings to mask the scent from patrol dogs."

"Interesting," Salazar remarked. He sat silently for a moment, and then said, "I tell you guys what. You cannot buy less than ten kilos of heroin and thirty kilos of cocaine per month." Salazar let that sink in. "For you, though, being a friend of Chino's, I'll charge you $5,000 per kilo for the cocaine. They are usually $2,000, but taking the credit card payment into account. The $3,000 is really of no financial burden, so the 150-percent mark-up is within your reach, friend. The heroin kilos are $15,000 each."

Kareem had one concern: Could Dre push that much dope?

"Let's do the math," Marquis said. "If the coke is sold at $22,000, that'll be $660,000 a month. Add that to $50,000 per key of dope, and that totals $1.6-million."

"We can do that," Kareem said, confident that Dre could make it happen with the help of Chino.

Salazar agreed, and stood and the three men followed him. Outside, he shook their hands and told them everything would be taken care of. He then told them to take one of his girls to chauffeur them around during their stay in Colombia.

CHAPTER 48

*T*he next day, Toi sat on the sofa and watched TV. After flipping through the commercials, she called Shimir.

After three rings, he answered. "What's up. Toi?" He asked, smiling at himself in a mirror. He loved when he was in control.

"Dang. How you know it was me?" she asked, realizing that she had forgotten to block her number the first time that she called.

"Come on wit' dat. Why you hollering at me so soon?"

"Well, Mr. All American is still in Colombia. I was thinking we could hang out."

"I must really be a tasty side order. What do I come with or without cheese?"

"Hopefully without," she said. "It's Monday night and I still have not saw *Cats*."

"*Cats!* I don't do musicals. Do that shit with dude." After a brief moment of silence, he said, "For you, though. Meet me at...Hold it. What time is the last show? It's already noon."

"Let's do the 7:30 show." Toi felt powerful having a say in what she did, as opposed to Kareem doing everything for her. She did appreciate a man that catered to her, Kareem was always ahead of the game.

"Why so late? Won't ol' boy be home tonight? Columbia can't be that far from where you live."

"I meant Colombia, the country, not the university." *How the fuck did he know, or guess that Kareem was a student at Columbia?*

"Plenty of time for us to get acquainted."

CHAPTER 49

*O*ver the next three days, the threesome navigated through Medellin easily. For Salazar to be a small guy, he had a lot of power. They had bought the warehouse and hired a staff to fully run the place. Marquis planned to have all of the equipment shipped, along with the finest silk, cotton, fur, and skin from around the world. Colombia was not all work, though. They had plenty of time to play. The American dollar and an association to Salazar were adequate to receive everything free, from dinner to pussy.

By day four, Dre wanted to get home to Tasha and Amare. Marquis had a woman, or two, that he wanted to get back too, as well. Kareem was not pressed one way or the other, he aggressively wanted to get the dollar on his team.

The three of them boarded a ten a.m. flight out of Colombia, headed for Miami International. During the flight, Kareem called Toi. He told her that, he would arrive in another day. He had every intention of surprising her.

*   *   *

*W*hen Toi hung up with Kareem, she smiled at Shimir. They were in Kareem's home; so, out of line.

Toi had hired the chef on duty in the building to prepare boneless chicken breast cooked in red wine with mushrooms, onion and bacon. Shimir liked the candlelit dining room The Mary J. album filled the air. He was in the mood, even though, this was his first time in her home. She was a Manhattan woman with brains. How good the brains really were, he sought to find out.

She fixed both their plates and the delicious scent filled the air.

"I'll assume you can manage to bless the food?" she asked.

"Of course not, you know gangsta's just dig in. No time for any extra."

"Boy, bow your head." She demanded, angry at his jejune remark.

They both bowed their heads, as she said a little prayer.

"Amen. Is this pork?"

"No, turkey bacon, boo," she replied.

After they ate, Toi covered the left overs, while Shimir put the dirty dishes in the dishwasher. He felt his phone vibrate against his hip and checked the text message. After he read it, he rushed toward the door. "I have to get out of here…"

*   *   *

"*N*ice roses, Mr. Bezel," the doorman said as Kareem emerged into the building's lobby.

"They are nice, huh? One for each day that, I have been away from Latoya," he told him smiling. He had picked up the flowers from the Miami airport.

"See Doug," an elderly tenant told her husband. "When was the last time you brought home flowers?"

"You spend my pension, social security and 401(k). Buy your own damn flowers."

Kareem shook his head and continued to the elevator. The elevator soared to his floor, and he thought lovingly about Toi. Would they be married with children at eighty? Spend months living in their Italy home? Be like the old couple that he passed.

When the elevator stopped on his floor, he grabbed his luggage and waited for the doors to open. When they did, Shimir was the only actor on the stage.

CHAPTER 50

He held his composure and walked past the bilious blackguard peacefully. Before the elevator door closed, he glanced back to get a better look. Sure enough, the derelict from the restaurant had received a call from Toi. He sat on his large suitcase and stared up at the ceiling.

How could she do this to me? I am a good man, lover and friend.

He thought long and hard. Firstly, it was quite ironic Shimir exited the loft as he arrived, especially since Toi expected him the next day. Secondly, the doorman's compliment of the flowers was strange. He pulled out his cell phone and dialed as he walked over to the window that overlooked Madison Avenue. He was angry, so fuck the lovely view of Central Park.

"Bezel residence," the maid answered. Kareem had hired the Asian maid to tidy up for Jean-Mary in his absence.

He responded somberly when Jean-Mary answered the phone. She could tell that something was wrong with him. "Now don't make me red-eye to New York. I hear the anguish in your voice."

"I have a major, no super-major problem."

"That ain't a word, but I'm all ears," she said, placing her hand on her hip.

"Remember the guy's number I told you that Toi took?" Kareem realized how stupid the question sounded after he completed it, but he was distraught. Jean-Mary recalled, and he said, "Well, sit down for this...He just walked to the elevator pass me."

"Where are you? Was Toi with him? Where is she now?"

"Are you ready for this?"

"Where boy?" she asked with an attitude. "My blood is simmering waiting to boil."

"The 15th floor of my building."

Jean-Mary let in a deep breath and Kareem heard the phone hit the floor. Jean-Mary gathered her composure and picked the phone up. "That bitch—Ooops—that harlot. How could she?"

"I have no idea. I'm devastated. All I wanted was to love her, Granny. She really crossed me."

"Now, you cross her. That's right! Cross her right on out of your life, baby."

CHAPTER 51

*K*areem *entered the loft and heard Beyonce blaring through the surround-sound* stereo. Toi was nowhere in sight. His heart pounded all over again. Was she hurt? Was she away and he broke in? Was he in another apartment and this was a coincidence? He set his bags down and walked past the kitchen. He took in a deep breath and stopped. Bone-colored china plates, gold flatware, and the building warmers sat on the table. She had invited him to dinner. *This woman is crazy*, he thought.

He continued down the hallway toward the steps that led to the loft. He approached the bathroom, and as the door opened, he heard the hum of the fan. Toi walked out, bumped into him and screamed as if she had seen a ghost.

"You scared the shit out of me," she said, and hugged him.

She dripped with diamonds. Really done from head to toe, for her little date. *All dressed for her boyfriend.*

"I guess, I did startle you. The door was unlocked and the music is loud as hell."

"I thought that I had locked it. I expected you."

She was such a liar. Or maybe she had expected him, having been tipped off by whoever warned the man to leave. "You look sexy as hell," Kareem told her, pulling her close. "Maybe, I need to go away more often." He planted soft kisses on her lips.

She kissed him passionately, and then told him to join her for dinner. "I had Jacques prepare your favorite for dinner, *coq au vin.* Hopefully it's not cold."

Not as cold as your lying ass. And I'mma get you.

CHAPTER 52

*K*areem *awoke refreshed after a long night of sexual pleasure with Toi. He* grabbed a shower and kissed her goodbye, before he hopped in a cab and headed to his bank job. Indeed it was a bank job. He arrived at his office, and as soon as he clocked in using his desktop computer, his bank manager and two unidentified men walked into his office. He was startled by the intrusion, but kept his cool. Not worried about a thing, even though, he thought that they were policemen.

He was right.

The men flashed their badges and introduced themselves.

He learned that they were from the Secret Service. "Oh, great! I guess this meeting is not a secret, though." *First, I'm loosing my bitch, and now this. What the fuck is my life becoming? It's crashing and burning piece-by-piece.*

"Neither is all of the money that you have been purloining. Stand up for me."

"For what? Am I under arrest?"

The man pulled out an affidavit to arrest Kareem Jamel Bezel. "You're definitely under arrest."

"Diane, what are they doing here?" Kareem asked the bank manager.

"You did not think that you could continue to get away with the things you have been doing here under my watch? Did you?"

"I have not committed a crime here!"

"Oh, cut the shit, mister. We have you and your accomplices stealing fiercely at Chase," said Agent Baine.

"Yeah, giving us their names and telling us how you all operate would look good to the US Attorney," said Agent Williams.

"Really," Kareem said, rubbing his goatee. "Too bad, I maintain my innocence."

"Come on. We have video surveillance of you and them taking down Chase. Clever costumes, I must say," Agent Baine said, pulling out a CD-book filled with DVD-R discs, which he claimed captured all of Kareem's actions.

"Lies and deceit. You have to wake up earlier in the a.m. to pull one over on me. Show me the CDs." Kareem was scared that hey may have not bluffed.

"We do not have to show you everything. Get it from your attorney with the rest of the discovery materials."

"Will I really need an attorney?" Kareem asked, acting dumbfounded. His brain worked feverishly in an attempt to figure out how much they really knew. Did they know about all of his actions, or just some of them.

"You betcha. Especially if you do not have any volunteer information for me. We know you have done things that we have no clue about," one agent said.

"You're quite clever, I must say," the bank manager said.

"Come clean and this could disappear," said the agent.

Damn, they're on my top. "What have I done? You're just talking, and have not showed me anything. I am beginning to resent the accusations absent proof. That is, if you have really made any accusations."

"If you do not intend to tell us anything, we may as well go ahead and take you to your one o'clock arraignment."

"Then we should be going. New York traffic is a bitch this time of day." Kareem's mouth was nasty, but he knew, he had a problem.

CHAPTER 53

After being arraigned on bank fraud and embezzlement charges, Kareem posted a $10,000 recognizance bail, and was told to report to the pre-trial services once a week until the outcome of his case. Rather than go home, he had needed to clear his mind, out of a cell. He had been arrested for robbing his job, which undoubtedly meant that he was also fired from his job. He surmised that his known accounts would be seized, but all he put in them was his paychecks. It would be an arduous task for law enforcement to track his overseas bread.

He sat in Section-26 of the Madison Square Garden, and watched with restrained excitement as the Sixers pounded on the Knicks. He often argued basketball with Knicks fans, but tonight there was no reason, too. He told them, "The Knicks have problems, but the Sixers have *The Answer.*"

Next to him was a sexy woman in a Knicks jersey dress. She held a cell phone to her ear and Kareem witnessed the lightened ring of skin around her ring finger. She had recently removed a wedding ring, had a chocolate complexion, and Kareem wanted to take advantage of her availability. At least for the night; he was too smart to have an affair. He wondered if he should tell Toi about his arrest. *Fuck outta here, that's just what I need, her, all up in my business.*

Out of boredom, he struck up a conversation with the woman next to him. Her name was Vivienne. She was a segment producer for a local news channel. After they had settled on a good conversation and exchanged numbers, Kareem's cell phone vibrated, and he answered it.

"Bjorn Prodigy, huh?" the familiar voice asked. Kareem was caught off guard. *My world is really coming to an end.*

Kareem frowned as if he had heard Satan. He backed away from Vivienne and shifted in his seat. In spite of his complexion, he morphed to pale. *This shit can't be happening*, he mumbled aloud.

"What's the matter, Prodigy? You looked vexed, fuming. You remember me, right? Agent Lucas McKenzey. I see the beads of sweat coming through that pin stripe."

Oh, shit. Kareem jumped to his feet.

McKenzey was close to him. Kareem looked around for his nemesis. He panicked. He made his way toward the Garden's corridor. In the phone, he said, "I knew you'd be coming."

"Here I am. I've never left, though. I allowed you to post bail. Because, boy do I have plans for you."

"You should not have." Kareem was racing toward the exits.

"Please! That sort of arrest was a little without confrontation, or embarrassment. You're going down, I assure you of that, but not that simply, *boy.*" McKenzey found that worthy of a chuckle. "You can't run. My men are covering every exit."

"Thanks. See you in traffic."

Kareem slammed his phone shut and peeled off his blazer to blend in with the crowd. At the end of a corridor, on the ground level was a door marked AUTHORIZED PERSONNEL ONLY. He hit the push-bar with his hip and walked inside.

The Garden security guards were inside the area smoking what Kareem knew was pot. He had interrupted them and they quickly extinguished their drugs after he told them that he was a DEA Agent looking for a quick way out to cut off a drug smuggling Jamaican.

Seconds to late, McKenzey's goons busted into the corridor with their pistols drawn. They reported to McKenzey that his most wanted had escaped.

CHAPTER 54

At seven-thirty p.m., Kareem met Marquis and Dre at the Petrie Court Café. The Metropolitan Museum was the perfect venue for them to draw a work of art to thwart McKenzey's wrath. Kareem informed them of his latest events, minus the detail about Toi's infidelity. He didn't feel like hearing any bullshit, as he laid down the new law.

"We have to cut our ties with anyone out of our circle, and this is the circle. Anyone else could be a McKenzey operative." Kareem let that sink in, and then said, "You're flings, too."

"Nigga are you crazy?" Dre asked, foolishly. Of all the things that Kareem said, all he was pressed about was pussy. "Leah is my main side bitch. There is no way that I am going to cut her off. She ain't working for that fag."

"We do not know that." Marquis said, quickly. He wasn't trying to hear shit.

"I've carried us this far, Dre, with wise decision making, and I have not dropped the ball yet."

"I can't tell."

"Don't be a smart-ass," Kareem said, warning him.

"She goes, period!" That was Marquis.

"Mind your fucking business. Ain't a period. Both you mutha-fucka's think that you can talk to me any kind of way."

Kareem raised his eyebrows and his jaw dropped, obviously insulted. He said nothing for a moment. After swallowing a gulp of water, he leaned back in his seat and tented his hands behind his head. "There are rules to this game and the agent is heavily favored to get the win. I knew telling you about my arrest and McKenzey's arrival into the future would cause you to panic a little and realize that we needed to switch the game up to adjust to this development."

"Don't fuckin' baby him, Reem," Marquis said. "He is letting pussy dictate his decision making. He can get down with the rules of this operation, or he can get the fuck out." Marquis let that sink in, and then said, "At his own risk."

"Pussy you threatening me?"

"Dawg, sit the fuck down and act like the fuck you know." Marquis stood and made it clear that Dre was not to be fooled by his smooth aura.

"I don't have time for this bullshit, with you nigga's. I'm outta here."

"He's right, Dre. You letting pussy—"

"Oh, so you're taking his side. Just how your father and mother takes your side all the time."

"This ain't about sides," Marquis said.

"You sound like a real bitch. What the fuck are you talking about?" Kareem asked. "You're a grown ass fucking man."

The last statement to Dre's back, as he walked out the restaurant.

CHAPTER 55

A week later, Dre rolled down the driver's window as he drove up the Schuylkill Expressway from his new Southwest Philadelphia secret bachelor pad. He and Chino were on their way to meet Ice. The night air seeped through the window and created a whistling sound as he sped 85 mph. The two street pharmacists rode in silence inside of a rented Silhouette mini-van.

Dre realized that he was wrong for walking out of that restaurant. He was equally wrong for letting seven whole days pass without kissing Kareem's ass with apologies. He was worried about Kareem, even though, he knew that Kareem was very capable of taking care of himself. Dre was obstinate, and he hated when his brother proved to be smarter than him. He now had to fend for himself. Kareem helped him think. He had already sold enough crack cocaine to get the ten-year minimum mandatory sentence. *No need to stop now,* he thought.

He reached 17th and Jefferson Streets and parked. Chino moved to the back seat, so that Ice could hop into the front. Ice passed a blunt to Chino. Dre did not smoke. Dre was not easily persuaded, so he never succumbed to the smoking frenzy. He couldn't adhere to his brother's wise advice, so peer pressure didn't fly either.

When Chino slammed the door shut, he asked, "Dre, whose briefcase is this back here." He held the case in the air.

"Leah's," he responded, confidently, but he looked at the case puzzled that she had forgotten it. He knew women played silly games, and felt that Leah left the case for Tasha to find. He was sure that Leah was not a McKenzey operative, but she was no less a monkey wrench. This had been the second thing that she left in his car. A hotel receipt with all of her personal data on it was the first.

After negotiating a deal for Ice to cop the first batch of dope from Dre, the men had stepped out the Silhouette to have a tester sample the pure Colombian product. Dre had Ice under the impression that he had Chino under his wing and that Chino had ripped off another drug dealer for the product. By Ice's estimation, if he had someone else's dope that was good and they had nothing: win-win.

The tester jogged into the crack house as happy as a pedophile in a school yard. All of the other feigns reacted, scattering about frantically, as they all knew the deal.

Suddenly, Dre fell to the ground and crawled under an abandoned car parked behind the minivan. The drive-by shooter's gun spat out rounds rapidly. Bullets ricocheted and penetrated the minivan in groups, not allowing room for a shoot-out.

Ice was pissed.

Dre was pissed.

The weapons used had a firing rate resembling a Cobra 12 gauge, viciously given the ghetto moniker, the "street sweeper."

Ice crawled to an abandoned house, narrowly escaping with a grazed shoulder. Crack-heads and corner boys dove to the ground and recited their *Our Fathers* and *Hail Mary's.*

Twenty seconds passed, and the power punch of the Cobra continued to spray gravel up under the car. The gunmen were not marksmen and the night darkness did not prove the best light. Yet, the bullets continued to pour. Dre lay there, wondering how long he would survive before the gunmen noticed that they were not being fired upon, get out of their vehicle, and start shooting directly at their targets.

The firing ceased when the car tires were heard racing off. The tires kicked shells under the car assaulting Dre. Good thing that they were not shot from a gun.

Dre pulled himself from under the car and found his orange Akademik sweat suit stained with oil and dirt. All of the Silhouette's windows were gone and the panels were severely penetrated. His body hurt badly, but Chino was in worse shape.

Chino held one hand on his chest and the other hand wrapped around his gun. He mouthed, "Dre, help me." He had been shot in the throat.

CHAPTER 56

Dre stuck the key in the ignition and turned it. The car started despite the heavy damage. He drove down Jefferson Street swerving and speeding. He prayed that he did not encounter any police cruisers. He had the perfect probable cause in the back seat to justify a search of the vehicle and seize the driver. In the distance, he heard the wail of sirens that raced to the crime scene he just departed.

At 17th Street, Dre turned right and continued to the hospital on the corner of 17th and Girard Avenue. When he crossed Girard, he drove past the hospital, though. He pulled over just passed the hospital and jumped out of the mini van. He climbed into the back seat and checked Chino for a pulse. There wasn't one.

He grabbed Leah's briefcase and Chino's gun and climbed out. He packed the drugs in his gym duffle bag after he took out his sweaty gym clothes. He took off the battery-included orange and put on his black Polo sweat suit, to which he ignored the smell of stinking sweat.

Dre walked from the car, but he returned, having forgotten an important piece of evidence to at least give the cops a hard time with figuring out who the car belonged to.

Dre strolled down Girard Avenue, and as he crossed 15th Street, a Chevrolet Caprice Classic passed him slowly. The driver yelled, "yo, get in!"

Dre continued to walk and crossed the street. He did not know the driver. He cut through the Kentucky Fried Chicken parking lot and was cut off by the Caprice that came whipping into another entrance of the parking lot.

Dre stuffed Chino's gun into the driver's window. "Who the fuck is you? Speak or I'll blow your fuckin' brains out!"

"Don't shoot," the man said. "I'm a criminal investigator. I work for an attorney, but was hired by your brother to keep an eye on you. I provided the information that got you off that Snobli murder. Please put the gun down and get the fuck in the car, before someone sees you and calls the police."

Dre ignored the man's advice and with his free hand he dialed Kareem. When Kareem picked up, he put the phone on speaker. "Talk to him."

"Kareem, I have Dre. He has a gun on me. He was shot at by three white guys in a black Navigator," the man said in one breath.

"Dre, that's Mr. Jonathan Rude. Get the gun off him and get the hell out of there, now!"

Obstinately, Dre stood there stunned. He did not have anything to say, and he was confused. "Where are you?" He asked his brother, and hopped into the Caprice.

Once again, saved by my little nigga, Dre thought.

CHAPTER 57

Cut hyacinths scented the air. Other than the television, only the rattle of the chip bag could be heard in the Lowes Hotel suite in downtown Philadelphia. Kareem's head rested against the hotel headboard. His face revealed his vulnerability to hurt and anguish. He laid across the bed, in quietude and pondered his fate. Dre's tirade had not overwhelmed him because his brother was not dead. What he watched on his laptop though was devastating.

Shimir was in his living room, again, this time pulling Toi close to him. Intimately. She ignored his intimacy and gave him a friendly hug. He pulled her in and tried to kiss her. This was what Kareem got for installing spy ware. He asked for this.

Shimir then grabbed Toi's arm violently and sunk his hands deep into her bicep, snatching her close to him. He pointed his index finger in her face, and fear swept across her face. He looked at her violently and then tossed her to the floor without words, before he stormed out the loft.

Kareem was mad at himself. He installed those cameras. Had he been in New York and not doing a trunk show at Neiman Marcus at King of Prussia mall, he would have been there, and not in a hotel chasing away his problems with vodka? Maybe, he didn't have to work so much, which alienated her to begin with. He felt dusky and responsible for her assault.

There was a light bang on his hotel room door and he checked the peephole before he let his brother in. The brothers hugged each other. The moment was surreal.

Tired of their embrace, Rude cringingly remarked, "Pull your selves together. We are still men here. Besides, you just had a gun the size of Texas in my face."

The brothers smiled and patted each other on the back.

Kareem told Rude, "You've done a fine job. Now get out of here."

"Are you sure?"

"Yeah, we'll be fine. I wanna get my life back tomorrow, though. I'll give you the details of what I need."

"And, I have the perfect way to handle this." That was Dre Bezel the Great. Finally he had a plan.

CHAPTER 58

The following day, mid-morning brunch was served to raucous hordes of downtown shoppers and the hospital workers at the Midtown II restaurant. It was nestled among the small stores across from the Thomas Jefferson Hospital. The sun beamed violently through the windows lighting the quiet corners of the café. While diners dashed in and out of the restaurant, a sinister meeting took place in the far corner.

"Let me be concise, here," McKenzey said his voice full of ire. "I asked you to track him. I figured you had mastered your craft. I thought of myself as lucky to have a former partner like you. Too bad they forced us to split up. But right now, Kareem's feeling like he can shock me at his discretion. And guess what, you have successfully raised his confidence by not killing Dre last night."

"Listen here, the outcome of this is the result of your ineptitude. Do not talk to me like I am one of your subservient thugs. You called me in to help you out. The self-proclaimed guru, the ayatollah. Don't exercise your jaw muscles to scold me again," Agent Belton said, unconcerned about McKenzey's problems.

"Can I take your order?" the waitress asked, stymieing Belton's view of the restaurant's entrance. McKenzey's back was to the entrance. The woman recorded their orders on her pad, and then stuffed her pen into her braided hair, before she said, "Coming right up."

"Who me?" Kareem asked the waitress, and then took a seat at the booth, entering the agent's purlieu. He had a sly, foxy grin on his face. While McKenzey's face exposed the haunting details of his flabbergast.

"Speak of the devil," McKenzey said.

"And the devil shall appear. You talked me right up," Kareem said, boldly. He was there to shock and administer a dose of fear to the agents. "So, what's up, boys?"

"Funny you ask. We were just discussing you going up," McKenzey said. "Up to the penitentiary."

"I bet you crawled here to work something out." Belton said, he did not believe the audacity.

"You can work yourself out of this conversation, flea!" Kareem said, quickly.

"Mac?" Belton started. "I could pummel him right here to avoid the headache."

"That wouldn't be wise. I promise that. I'll remind you of your high school bully. All cops had one, pussy!"

Belton jumped to his feet in an attempt to intimidate. Kareem was faster and more agile, with no sign of fright. The two men breathed in each other's face.

"Belt, why don't you let me have a chat with, Mr. Bezel?" McKenzey had a sneer plastered on his face, but he had to diffuse the situation. He died to know how that encounter was brought to life.

"Are you sure?" Kareem asked. "The last time we were in private, you do remember what happened?" Kareem let that sink in and then asked, "You do know the score?"

Belton looked at McKenzey and huffed in disgust as he left the table.

"I'll be straight forward," McKenzey said.

Kareem cut him smooth off. "You're not in a position to speak first. I come to find some common ground between us."

"If you ever find it, it will no longer be common," McKenzey responded, staring into Kareem's cold eyes. He sipped his coffee.

"Mac—it's o'right for me to call you Mac, right?" Kareem asked, politely and went on. "You're not starting off on the right foot. I am here to make an offer. I'm willing to pay you to back off, but I want all of the intelligence that the feds have on me and my brother at your 6th Street haven for pigs. You know, over there at the year long cock-sucker's convention."

"You're this year's key note speaker. Here's some advice for you. My loyalty cannot be bought."

"A quick wit for an asshole. You're a strange one to mention price with all of the back pockets your hands have dipped into." The waitress placed two steak dishes in front of them, interrupting Kareem. She disappeared, and he continued, "To get us on the same course, I'll tell you that I've learned you thrive on terrorizing the weaker and more cowardly. You're weak and ineffectual, though." He paused, taking a stab into Belton's medium-rare porterhouse. He chewed the steak, dabbed his mouth with a napkin, and raved, "This is good," as if nothing happened.

"I have better things to do than play with you."

"Well let's cut to the chase. I plan to go to the public with the information that I have on you—" McKenzey tried to speak, but Kareem wasn't having that. He was taking this show to a dramatic climax. "I will pay you to disregard the information in exchange for the investigative notes and files from any policing agency regarding me or my brother. This *quid pro quo* comes with a million dollar bounty attached. Half now, and the otha half when you deliver. Or you can exchange tossed salad in prison with a man that looks like Shaq, but named Tiny."

"Foreplay like this only leads to sex. I am not that egregious. However,"—he pulled out a tape recorder—"I could arrest you for this chicanery. But I won't. I'd like it much better snatching you off a Bryant Park runway during fall fashion week."

"I don't mean to rape the thunder from your confidence, but you're not in control. I know what you did to my father, bitch ass cracka!"

"Our business is done. Obviously my last statement eluded your high fashion IQ. I am a decorated officer and I have the connection complexion. Don't-fuck-with-me."

"Check please," Kareem yelled to the waitress, as he left McKenzey at the table.

McKenzey laughed at the kid's tenaciousness.

* * *

McKenzey left a $5 tip on the table, and then used an ATM in the diner to withdraw cash to cover the tab. He obtained forty bucks and checked his balance. He scanned the receipt, and something came over him. He had a burning desire to get the fuck out of America and pound the pavements of some foreign city. Five minutes earlier, he felt up for the continued Bezel challenge, but after discovering $500,000 extra in his bank account, he wanted to wave the white flag.

At that moment McKenzey's cell phone rang. He answered and Kareem said, "Guess, I'm laughing now, bitch-ass clown!"

CHAPTER 59

While Kareem handled McKenzey, Dre was in the Bad Lands to set the wheel on motion to avenge Chino's death. The cops hadn't progressed in handling that job the legal way and the Colombian community was outraged. Local papers accused the police of abandoning the Hispanic Community. The police had a few dots; none of them connected. Without someone pointing the finger at the shooters, their investigation was as moot as the 9/11 Commissions—no one claimed responsibility for that attack.

Pretty Tony introduced Dre and Benjamin, and then he ran down the math to get back at the clowns that killed Chino, hood style. Ten minutes later, Dre was in Benjamin's living room.

"I'm going to need you butter ball naked." Ben told his guest, exhibiting why he was called Ben Laden. His circle was tight and anyone attempting to get in for whatever reason had to play by his rules.

Dre snapped out of his mystified state. Back to reality, he looked bemused. Rather than question, though, he complied, down to his boxers. Ben kicked his clothes toward the kitchen and used his gun to point at Dre's boxers, then towards the floor. Refusal to recognize the authority figure in this case would be disastrous. Dre did not want to bear all. It appeared his hands were tied and he would have to submit.

With his penis out the bag, Dre watched in dismay as his clothing was picked up, taken to the kitchen sink and dumped inside. Ben removed the currency and a brown wallet from Dre's jean pocket. He then reached for the spigot and drowned Dre's clothes. Ben returned to the kitchen and sent Dre upstairs to get a change of clothing. Anger was on Dre's mind, but he regarded the thugs of the Bad Lands as good and conscientious men, who were notorious for getting away with crimes.

Dre returned downstairs and got straight to the point. "How much to do an Italian?"

"Depends? How you want him done?"

CHAPTER 60

Hours later, Kareem parked in front of 757 Madison Avenue. He nodded at his doorman and scanned the lobby. Struck by the lobby's luminous quality, Kareem suddenly appreciated the Van Gogh paintings lining the Carrara marble corridor that led to the elevators.

"Toi! Sweetheart, I'm home," Kareem shouted as he shut and locked the loft door behind him.

There was no response. He heard soft music playing. The music came from the living room. He traced Ginuwine's voice, a track from his album titled, *The Senior*. He followed the smooth balladeer to the living room, and found Toi on the sofa.

She was startled by Kareem's early arrival home and suspiciously hid something behind her back. He witnessed her surreptitious behavior and his excitement to see her had morphed into a distrustful sleuth.

She hoped that he did not recognize her movements and cheerfully greeted him. "Hey baby! I'm glad your home. I've missed you like crazy."

He stood in front of her with his face twisted in disgust. "Oh! You did, huh?" He asked and recalled her moment with Shimir. He tried to desperately keep his cool before he confronted her. But all of his stuffed heartbreak swam to the surface, and he could not tolerate her flagrant disrespect anymore; but, he did not want to reveal his hand just yet. He swallowed the lump in his throat and pretended to be just as elated to see her. Toi flung her arms open, inviting him into her space, but remained seated.

Kareem held his ground. "No! Get up, so I can squeeze that...," he told her, and gawked lustfully at her ass.

Toi smiled wildly, but he did not get up. "Baby, I'm tired, because I've been at the doctor's all morning. Add to that, I'm comfortable. So, come over here." She demanded, and then sealed it with, "Ple-e-e-e-ase."

He did not care about her sexy, innocent look. He was adamant that she stand. He had McKenzey to deal with, along with a host of other mundane things to tend to. He would not deal with her nonsense. "Doctor's office? What's wrong with you?"

The way he asked the question, offended her. "Nothing's-wrong-with-me! I, uh, just went to see my gynecologist for an exam," she said, looking at the ground.

"What the fuck you got? For your sake—"

"I don't have shit," she said interrupting him. "You gave me something."

Kareem could not fight the devil off his back. "What, bitch? What the fuck could I have given you?" He yelled and hesitated, before slamming her with a powerful thunder of verbal insults. "You have been having a sordid relationship with that hood nigga, and you probably got something from him. What, you don't think that these walls or the streets talk?"

"But, Kareem—"

"Don't interrupt me when I am fucking talking. I've had enough of your bullshit. I work hard and you fucking complain. You had the audacity to have that nigga up in my crib, too." He ended his rant and walked over to the bar and poured himself straight 151-proof vodka.

She cringed with each word that he yelled. She got herself together and looked forlornly. "You're one-hundred-percent right. This is an opulent lifestyle. It's packed with high fashion, amazing parties, and smooching celebs. That's all dandy, but—"

"I'm not tryinna here this bullshit," he said and sipped his cocktail.

"Let me finish. That's all gravy, but all I want is you. Yes, I have been hanging with a male, but I saw him as a friend. He tried to kiss me and when I pushed him away, he bruised me." She removed her jacket and revealed the mark that Shimir had left. "I need a male friend. Like the old Kareem Bezel used to be. Not like that all-important, millionaire-influenced, workaholic Bjorn Prodigy." She sounded as if she had rehearsed those lines for weeks.

He sat his glass down and clapped his hands. "And the Academy Award for Best Actress in a Cheating Thriller goes to..." He sipped his drink, and then walked toward her. "Listen carefully, no one will invent a copy machine with a feature to replica me. I cannot believe you have such a hard time accepting my ambition. That's just too bad because, I promised myself that I would take care of myself and my family with my intelligence. Simple as that! So can that bullshit. You're here, or you're not." He paused to sip his drink, and then politely asked, "What's behind your back?"

"I don't have anything behind my back." She again whined, as she sat back deeper into the sofa and wiggled around in an attempt to further conceal the item.

"I don't believe that you have the audacity to lie to me, Toi," he told her, pulling a 9x11 gift-wrapped box from behind her back. He unwittingly went on to scold her, as he snatched the paper off the gift. "What's this for that nigga? You have to wake up at the crack of dawn to pull one over on me. You thought that you were getting over on me. Little Bobby next door already alerted me to your cheating. He asked if I knew your brother. I didn't know you had one. But if he's your brother, what the fuck am I?"

"A father!" she said, as he pulled a book from the box.

CHAPTER 61

Tears fell from her eyes. It seemed like, she walked through a rainstorm. The words were more powerful than President John Adams' Inaugural Address on March 4th, 1797, that included a 727-word sentence.

Kareem read the title of the book: *Pregnancy Sucks, For Men* by Kimes & Kimes. He flipped to the first page and read the inscription:

Dear Reem:

> *Thanks for an incredible life, and I apologize for my selfish behavior. Now give me some love, and as you can see I am dressed for our party for three reservations at Per Se.*

Love Always,

Latoya

The room was silent, except for the noise made by Toi's nylon blouse when she handed him her home pregnancy test. Kareem fell back and knocked a Swarovski crystal swan off the end table. Glass shattered everywhere. He sat in awe. He had been so busy that he had missed the good things. For a change he was lost for words, in a state of confusion. He felt like dancing down the toilet along with all of the excrement that had just dropped out of his mouth. He tried to put a string of ideas together. Opting for the obvious, he hugged her, and she sank deep into his arms.

"I had to see my GYN because I have missed my period for a month. She set me up to get a test in her lab, but I couldn't wait, so I spent $200 at Duane Reade to buy a home test."

Kareem slouched with her wrapped in his arms. He was bewildered. He had not digested everything and felt uncomfortably ashamed of his actions. A tsunami of emotions hit him hard. He had no idea what to do, so he relinquished his emotions with tears.

There was nothing to be said, other than, "You have no idea how much I love you, Toi. This is about far more than running around with celebrities. More than traveling here and there. I want so much to please you and to really change the lives of the people around me. I work hard for myself of course, but the visions of the end result for my family is on my mind every step of the way."

"I know baby, and that's why I love you so much. I knew that this was your plan in high school, so why I've been so selfish is beyond me. Everyone that I encounter sums up your qualities as a superior man—even my damn gynecologist, for Christ's sake, she read about you in the Times. I do not want to lose you. I am sorry for going behind your back and fraternizing with someone else. I assure you that it was harmless and nothing sexual ever happened."

"Toi, do not lie to me. The last thing that I need is for a nigga to come up on me and claim that he was fucking you, while I ran around trying to get life better for you."

"Kareem, please don't do this. I did not do anything sexual with him..." She paused and leaned to grab the stereo remote. She raised the volume of the stereo, which played Ginuwine singing a song about his first born. She told Kareem to listen to the song.

The song played, and Toi's actions gradually vanished into Kareem's memory. He did not want their love to fail. Especially not then, as his career ballooned to stardom. He needed to be loved. Needed someone there. He needed Toi.

She moved her body to become face-to-face with him. Her breath tinged with peppermint, as they kissed. She leaned back and he climbed on top of her.

CHAPTER 62

*L*ater, the night air whistled, but was barely heard with the Tupac lyrics shouting through the stereo system. The system was not loud enough to alert neighbors to their presence, but it was loud enough to pre-hype Dre and Ben Laden. They needed to feel Tupac's music. Feel the legend's pain. Gangster music catapulted Dre's mood from anxious to deadly.

Dre parked the car in the middle of a row of cars in front of a row of condos. The gray homes were large, many of them with floor-to-ceiling sliding doors, connecting the small patio areas to the living room. Easy access to the homes. Their private spaces. Their precious jewels. Only one condo was of interest to Dre: Brent Gower's.

They took precautions in order to commit the perfect burglary. There would be no DNA, fingerprints, or footprints left behind to connect them to their home invasion. They approached the screen door and Ben Laden used wire cutters to snap the bolt and padlocks from the door. Dre pulled the door handle and the door slid back.

They stepped inside.

* * *

*A*n hour later, Brent pulled into his usual parking space in front of his condo. He casually stepped out the truck as Carmen followed. He pulled her close to him and wrapped his arm around her, whispering sweet sexual quips into her ear.

They pounded the gravel under their feet until they reached the storm door. Brent fumbled with the keys before he opened the screen door. He inserted another key into the door's dead bolt and found it unlocked. He would have never failed to secure his home.

"Did you lock the door before we left?" He asked her accusingly.

"You locked up. I was just about to ask you the same thing," she responded, and seemed offended.

He turned the door knob and walked through the doorway. He felt along the wall for the light switch and in an instant his heart pulsated.

The VCR clock was not on and he saw metal glistening where the 60-inch plasma was.

"What the hell? You have got to be kidding me," Carmen said, when he flipped the light switch on.

BG stood in the doorway. He was heated. He observed his ransacked sanctuary. Was anyone still in his home? Had he caught them in the act? Carmen grabbed BG for protection, but he pulled away from her, and ran over to the broken urn on the floor by the fireplace. He grabbed a handful of his grandfather's ashes. They reeked or urine.

"I'm calling the cops!"

BG jumped up and snatched the phone from her hand.

"But, BG, you were robbed. The police would—"

"Shut up! Please! Listen, let me do this. I know who f

"What if this was random? You really need to report

"Look, I do not need you to talk right now. Go the days clothes. I got to get out of here for a few days."

BG went into the kitchen to get the Crock-pot wi planned to remove the cash and put his grandfather's ashes was gone, so he returned to the living room and used a sp from the floor. Carmen came out of the bedroom, luggage in

* * *

BG and Carmen pulled up to the Roosevelt Inn, a sorry motel on the Roosevelt Boulevard stretch of Route 1. BG wanted to go down a little further to a fancier hotel, but Carmen did not think that was a good idea with him having a gun.

After they checked in and entered the room, BG placed his loaded gun on the night table. He stripped down to his boxers and turned down a hideous comforter before he slipped under it.

He lay in bed and looked at the TV, as Carmen undressed down to her panties and bra set. She left her clothes on the floor near the bed, and slowly switched across the front of the bed to turn off the room light. When she turned around, she slipped off her bra. His eyes caught her model figure and he became mesmerized. She smiled back at him like a kid caught stealing a car.

She climbed under the sheets and whispered to him, "I know I could get your mind off this drama. Even if for a minute."

She then placed kisses with her warm lips onto his small, erect penis. He was turned on, but she wasn't. She could only take but so much, considering she was only with him for his money. She licked the shaft, and then circled the head much like she'd do a Tootsie Pop. He began to pulsate and she inserted him into her mouth. She probed fast, slow, in circles, and hard. She did not even gag and that irritated her. All of ninety-four seconds later, he was done. He squirmed and tried to get away from her jaws, which were still on him, sucking him dry. She drained him to the last drop. Unable to take it any more, he pulled her head off him. She wiped around her mouth with her fingers and then sucked them.

He immediately crashed to sleep, and she rolled out of bed. She grabbed her cell phone, and slipped into the bathroom.

CHAPTER 63

*M*oments later, the sound was deafening. The motel door swung open with a devastating crash and two masked men entered. With lightening-fast speed, BG reached for his gun and trained it on the two masked intruders, who also had guns drawn. Big guns, with silencers.

Carmen sat up on the bed, and pulled back the sheets over her breasts. BG sat up stupefied. He did not want to make any whimsical moves to anger the intruders. He thought who ever these guys were they probably just wanted money. Their actions were marked by brilliance and he desired to know who the masked men were. He gathered mettle and sat there sure the men only wanted money.

"We finally meet again." One of the masked men said. BG instantly recognized the voice.

"Last meeting, too, my nigga," Ben Laden said.

"This is how it's gonna end."

Dre removed his mask and the former partners were face-to-face. They analyzed their dilemma, and recalled the other's bad deeds. One of them would be quashed in that room. Maybe, both of them.

"Carmen, I suggest you get out of harm's way," Dre said.

BG delivered a crashing blow to Carmen's face. He should have known that she was a snake. She reached to catch the blood leaking from her lips, as BG wrapped a bicep around her throat, choked her, and then put his gun to her temple. The adroitness of his move impressed Dre, but he remained placid. "This little bitch set me the fuck up, huh?" She scratched at his arm, and fought to catch her breath.

"Your nut ass wouldn't be shit without me," said Dre.

"I'm the fucking quarterback, remember? I lead. I direct. I put you on the game, faggot!"

"Now, I'm the FedEx of Cocaine."

"I'mma kill this bitch," BG said, squeezing harder on her throat.

"Let her go, BG, before—"

"Before what, pussy?" BG jerked and flung Carmen to the floor. He squeezed off a shot aimed at her head. Nothing happened. A click and rotation of the barrel. He tried to shoot again.

Carmen gained her breath and composure. She then reached into her toiletry bag, jumped up, and threw bullets hard into BG's face. "I'm thinking you're gonna need these," she said, massaging her throat.

"Just kill me already," BG said, looking at Dre. The words suggested dejection and gloom. "Can you fucking kill me, please?"

That was a catchy request that Dre intended to fulfill, but not at that moment. It provoked the answer, "No, how many bullets did Chino get popped with? Six, mutha fucka. You got at least double that coming."

Ben Laden shot BG in the leg. "Startin' with that one."

CHAPTER 64

*I*mmediately after handling BG, Dre headed back to New York City. Not long after he arrived there, and he went to bed, an intruder lay in wait in his back yard. The man—over-dressed in army fatigues and knee high boots—sweltered in the summer heat. His dark brown eyes with rings around them confirmed a day wasted waiting for Dre's arrival. The man had no desire to kill Tasha and Amare without the man of the household present.

Abusing Dre was chancy, but the man planned to make Kareem Bezel pay, slowly for being savvier, shrewder, and suave than his pal, Agent Lucas McKenzey. The man desperately wanted to get Kareem, but he would need a more sophisticated means to get in and out of Kareem's building. Right now, Dre would pay for the raking pain caused by the nomenclature: The Bezel Brothers.

Thirty minutes passed since Dre turned off the bedroom light. The man was antsy. He pulled open the screen door and turned the doorknob. That was a surprise, he thought. The screen door was unlocked. Agent Turner retrieved a set of keys from his pocket. The one coded green fit into the top lock. The yellow one slid easily into the middle lock. And the red key fit snugly in the doorknob lock. He turned the knob and entered the home's kitchen.

* * *

*D*re's silent alarm alerted him on his bedside panel that he had a door ajar. He grabbed his Magnum from the night stand and switched the monitor to the kitchen. Dre signaled for Tasha to stay quiet in the bedroom, as he raced to grab Amare. Amare wrapped his arms around his father and rested his head on his shoulder. The baby was oblivious to the invasion.

Dre handed Amare to Tasha, who looked deathly afraid, and for good reason: someone had forcefully entered her home. Dre whispered into her ear, and they both reacted. Despite her fright, she was sure that Dre would spare nothing to protect her and their son.

* * *

*T*he unwanted man waited in the kitchen. He could not believe that the home owners had not responded to his disrespectful entry into their abode. They should have commanded the police to their home, but they were sound asleep. *Stupid ingrates,* he thought. The man treaded lightly, as he progressed into the suburban home. His Glock drawn in the event Dre decided to confront him with a sudden move. The man knew the brothers intimately, and he would kill Dre that night, he thought.

At the top of the spiral stair case, the man scanned the hallway, and noticed that the master bedroom door was partially open. The sneer on his face was repulsive. He wanted to see the state of shock, internal strain, and disbelieving stares on the homeowner's face. At the bedroom door, he slowly pushed it open. No creak. A good, rich door. Both of the brothers moved from Philadelphia and lived richly. Why did they deserve their lifestyles? He wanted a slice of the loaf, and that night, he planned to take a part of the green-colored bread.

When he reached the head of the bed, he positioned himself and placed his gun an inch from the heads under the blanket. He cocked his gun, and Dre with hurricane speed raced out his closet and offered the butt of his gun to the back of the intruder's head. The man fell forward and squeezed off a shot, as he lost the gun. Glass shattered from the framed picture on the wall, as Tasha bravely raced down the stairs with Amare.

The intruder attempted to stand as Dre delivered a kick to his face. And another to his gut, as Tasha reappeared in the bedroom. The man turned and saw that she had a gun trained on him. She said, "Please move, pussy! Please! God, I dare you to make one fuckin' move!" The man tried to speak, but Tasha screamed, "Shut the fuck up, pussy," before she shot him in the thigh.

"Don't! I'm a federal agent. My badge is in my wallet."

"I don't give a—" Tasha began, prepared to shot him again.

"Wait, Tash!" Dre yelled. "We might need this nigga."

* * *

Twenty minutes later, Kareem and Toi approached Dre's front door, as Tasha opened it. Tasha stepped aside, as they marched past her, both lured by the thought of who Dre and Tasha had bound and gagged in their family room.

When they reached the family room, Toi wanted to run away. Kareem's face became flushed with anger, and his sudden desire to be there had faded quickly. He could not believe that he stared at the face of, Shimir.

CHAPTER 65

*U*nder the early morning dawn, McKenzey pulled into the Roosevelt Inn parking lot, and found the boys-in-blue, milling about investigating a crime scene. He parked his car and jumped out. He flashed his badge to a young corporal, that guarded the crime scene before being waved in.

"So, besides my name being smeared in blood on the mirror, what do we have?" McKenzey asked the scene lieutenant.

Lieutenant Wong was a 13-year veteran, with his hair parted down the middle and he weighed in at 120-pounds. He would have made a lovely jockey.

"We have your star witness in a very compromising situation," Lt. Wong said, as they walked toward the room. "Brent Gower has been the canvas of an artistic buffoon. The techs are looking for prints and hair fibers. Video feed from the front desk was taken by the killers. The maid found him and is in the office hysterical. Second body she's found this morning. She went to the dumpster to hurl and found a woman inside dead with a single gun shot to the head."

"What was done to him?" McKenzey asked, eagerly walking to the room. He wanted the luxury of laughing inside at what was done to the simpleton. He wished that he had done BG in himself. He'd have too take his frustrations out on the Bezel brothers.

"It's a glimpse of a twisted predator that the guys in Quantico would adore to interview for behavioral science text books. This crime is like a grain of sand on the beach, very original, and just out right obnoxious."

"That damn smell is horrific."

"That's your guy's new body fragrance," Lt. Wong said, as they entered the room. He showed McKenzey the body and said, "The razor-like cuts on his arms appear to be done with a whiz-wheel that was purposefully left behind, I'm sure. It's bagged and tagged."

"You mean the high-speed cutter used to cut through car metal. You got to be fucking kidding me?"

"That's nothing. Check this out," Lt. Wong said and pointed to one of the cuts. "This one was re-closed with a propane torch. Also B&T. The pliers found to crush his testicles, too. And I assume the whiz-wheel removed his penis before it was implanted into his eye socket. That's just conjecture, don't quote me on that."

"This shit is sick. Don't believe it."

"How will this affect your case?" Wong asked icily. "He was your star witness against the Bezel's right? I heard that from a reporter over there."

McKenzey walked up to the camera man and snatched the recorder from the photographer and slammed it on the asphalt. "I'm sorry, but this story cannot be put on the air waves."

The aquiline, jovial reported lost it. "Why the hell not? This has aired live already. It's news and I deal in the business of airing news, Agent McKenzey."

"You just ruined my two-year investigation of a notorious crime family," McKenzey said, ignoring the fact, the reporter knew his name.

"D-E-A Agent Lu-cas Mc-Kenzey, what a character you are. I know all about your investigation, and I hardly call the Bezels notorious. I do know that for the sake of taking down two boys, neither of them 25-years-old, you've had a lengthy number of murders happen under your watch, including this one here. All to build a racketeering case and possibly get a Colombian, which you don't have one solid piece of evidence on, and you had the poor Brent Gower prepped to lie in order to get a conviction. This criminal system is so twisted. It allows all of these murders and kids to be abandoned to drug addicted mothers, while you wait to get the bigger fish, instead of getting dealers off the street ASAP."

"Enough of this," McKenzey said, and replayed all of the dead bodies in his mind. They started with Snobli, the Councilman, and now Brent "BG" Gower. He stormed from the scene and hopped in his car, as his cell phone rang. He pressed the TALK button and said, "Turner did you get them."

"Naw, we got Turner mutha fucka! You're next," the caller said, and hung up.

CHAPTER 66

Around six p.m., Leah was back in her apartment after a long day at work. She vanished into the bathroom, showered, and as she toweled off her door bell rang. It was Dre.

"To what do I owe this honor?" she asked nonchalantly. "What wifey left you, for running the streets?"

Dre ignored that. "Can I come in? I really need to talk to you."

She moved to let him in and locked the door behind him. He stood in the entryway and waited for her next move, as he stared at the contours of her body in her robe. She walked toward her bedroom. Like a dog in heat, he chased behind her, and enjoyed the provocative dance that her ass performed. He took a seat on her bed as she stood in the mirror and brushed her damp hair.

"So, you've been quiet enough. What are the odds of you needing to talk to me, especially after you just vanished without a word?" She asked with a hand on her hip.

"I had my reasons, but I mainly wanted to protect you. I need your help."

"Well, I knew that could be the only reason you were here. Typical!"

"Would you quit it? I never intended to hurt you. What I did was for your protection, trust me."

"Listen to me, carefully. When I told you, I was a federal employee. Did you think that I lied?"

"No, but joking, though. I didn't take you serious, but my brother had an investigator check you out."

"And he found that I am the deputy clerk for Judge Ruley. No big deal."

"It is, and I really need you."

"Let me hear what you could possibly need from me."

"I don't beat around the bush—"

"You beat up this bush," she said interrupting him, and grabbing his dick.

Not persuaded to get off base, he went on, and said, "I need to pay off a judge or prosecutor to botch our trial. Can you make that happen?"

"Now, why the hell would I do that for you, after you lied to me?"

"Don't make me beg. You remember what happened the last time that I had to get on my knees to beg?"

"Don't flatter yourself. I know the people to make it happen, but that ain't cheap. I'll have to look into it."

"We are ready to pay what we weigh, and of course, this is for you to begin looking," he said, and went into his jacket pocket and pulled an envelop out. He gave it to her, and said, "Ten-thousand and much more where that came from."

She tossed the money onto her dresser, and said, "Know for the record that you hurt me badly. I fell for you, and you crushed me." She stepped within an inch from him and untied her robe. Her two perfectly grown cantaloupes fell out; her nipples tumescent with anticipation. She leaned toward him, and rested her hands on his shoulders. Her gaze was gorgeous and uncritical. "You can apologize anytime now."

CHAPTER 67

Kareem could not gather himself to leave his office, but that changed with a call from his grandmother' maid.

"LuAnn, is there a problem?" he asked, urgently. Eight-thirty at night, there was no reason for LuAnn to call him.

"Mr. Bezel," she said, cautiously. "I arrived at Granny Jean-Mary's late, as you requested, and—"

"What! I didn't request shit." He was haplessly upset and did not wish to use foul language, but he was shook up. A lone tear fell from his eyes, and he hadn't even heard anything bad. He felt it, though.

"The agency called me at home and told me that I should arrive late because you were taken her out to a doctor appointment."

"I didn't. Where's my grandmother, right now?" He asked, point blank.

"The house is..." she began.

"LuAnn!" He screamed. "Where the fuck is my grandmother?" Now he was pissed, and panicked. *I'm ready to fuck this dizzy bitch up.*

"The house is ransacked and she's not here."

"Nooooooooooo!" He yelled, as he raced onto the elevator to exit his building. He gathered what ever control he had, and asked her if she had her cell phone. "Call the police, now!" He then used the conference call feature on his cell phone and called Dre when he reached the lobby. He passed the security, and told Dre on the phone, "Go to Jean-Mary's ASAP!"

"Okay. Okay. What's up?" He asked, rolling from on top of Leah.

"She's gone. The..."

* * *

Dre heard the phone bounce along the pavement and waited a second. Dre did not know that Kareem slammed to the ground and onlookers threw themselves to the ground, as well to escape being shot. After fifteen seconds and no more shots, Kareem—barely conscious—grabbed the phone and cradled it to his ear.

"Dre, they shot me. Help Jean..."

CHAPTER 68

*D*re could not bare the thought of losing his brother or his grandmother. They were both vital to his existence. The lives of two people that he loved were in danger, and he was suddenly forlorn. He pulled himself together and prepared to score one for the team. Not a home run, but a grand slam. Relatives and friends suspected that he always depended on Kareem, but with Kareem out of the game, he planned to carry them to the championship parade.

He parked on the corner of Jean-Mary's block. He was unable to drive up her block because it was blocked by several police cars and an ambulance. An ambulance was all bad. He walked up the block, ignoring the neighbors who watched him intently. By now, they all knew what had happened, and he didn't.

He reached Jean-Mary's lawn and was questioned by the rookie officer covering the home. He explained who he was, and Sergeant Brown, the lead officer signaled for him to be let through. He approached the sergeant and hoped to get answers.

"This is not a crime scene. You can enter, but beware."

"Beware of what?" Dre asked, pushing past the detective.

"This," the slender cop told him, as he looked at the anger in Dre's eyes.

"What the fuck is this?" Dre screamed at LuAnn. She stood with a female officer who took a report from her. Dre was sickened by the sight of the living room, and could not fathom looking further. He turned to LuAnn.

"I have no idea. When I came over, I found the place all ransacked like this. I called Kareem, but we were disconnected, and when I tried to call him back, his recorder picked up."

The mention of Kareem's name brought up another situation. Dre was plagued by dilemma after dilemma. How was his brother, his pal? Was he dead? In a morgue? Still pressed to the street? So many questions, and so little time to answer them. "Did my grandmother have plans to be out that you know of?"

"Not to my knowledge. I asked Kareem about a call made to the service regarding him taking her out and for me to come here late. He denied making the call."

Dre turned to the cop. "You heard the woman. Someone lied to get her here late. My grand mom has been kidnapped."

"First of all, calm down, sir," Sergeant Brown told him. "There was no forced entry. We scanned the house and her diabetic medicine is gone. For all we know, she went out and someone did this while she was gone, and she'll be walking up the block any minute now."

Dre let out a deep breath and sighed. "Listen here, brainiac." He paused to gather himself. "If she went out, naturally she took insulin. But she would have returned earlier, and definitely told my brother. She's missing, I feel it." The policeman tried to get a word in, but Dre snapped. "Don't fucking cut me off! I know my grandmother. She would not be out without calling my brother, period. We are all she has, despite her many children."

The cop assured him that he was getting nowhere. "I understand your faith, but we have to wait at least 48-hours before she can be officially reported missing." The words rained on Dre with dismal gloominess.

"Then she's been missin' 50-hours officer."

"Are you suggesting, I—"

"Lie! Precisely." Dre snapped. "You know what, you act like you cannot lie, or do something. I bet if you were at a robbery scene and had an innocent man in custody, you'd lie about it." He was tired of explaining himself, so he said, "There was no crime. You can leave, now. You're trespassing!"

"What do you mean?"

"Get the fuck out!"

CHAPTER 69

*K*areem came through after being sedated, looked around the dreary hospital room. He felt an IV in his hand and rated that as the lowest level of pain. His upper torso screamed for narcotics to take away the twinge.

"You're alive. Thank you, Jesus!" Toi, by his side, looked up at him and confirmed for him that he was alive. She cautiously hugged him.

With slurred speech, he told her, "I love you. And the baby, too."

Good, she thought. His memory was fine. She thought that he was in a coma and possibly a vegetable, despite the physician drilling into her brain that he would be fine, when the morphine wore off. He suffered a shot to his clavicle, which pierced his humerus. They were in bandages.

He fought for the strength to ask the question of the day. "Where's my grandmother?" He scratched from morphine.

She explained what Dre had informed her regarding the altercation at Jean-Mary's. Darnell gathered all the strength, he could to sit up. *Good,* he thought, *despite my legs being wobbly. They still work.*

"What are you doing?"

"I gotta get to my grandmother, before the police get to me with questions about who shot me." With each move he made, the pain killed him, but he needed to help Jean-Mary. "I don't even know who did this." He could not let her down. There was no way that he would rest with her nowhere to be found. Pain or not, as long as he could walk and shoot a gun with his good right hand, he was leaving the hospital.

"Kareem, Dre has everything under control."

Bullshit. "Where are my clothes, Toi? This ain't up for discussion."

"Kareem, are you kidding me?"

He spotted his clothes and told her to help him put on his clothes. "I'm out of here. If you try to stop me, you can get away from me, too. I have to find my grandmother, and you now damn well, I ain't gonna stay here." He was so upset that he pounded the bed.

"Kareem, you can't leave. Please, listen to me. There's…"

Kareem grabbed onto the bed rail and climbed out of it. He tip toed and winced in pain from each step. He made his way to the door, in the hospital gown. *The hell with clothes. No one is gonna stop me, and Toi knows that!*

He reached the door and cringed from the pain, and the bright lights that shone in from the corridor. He tried to unfold the wheelchair that leaned against the wall. Toi looked on and wondered where he got the strength. He sat in the wheelchair and struggled to open the door. It opened. He rolled out into the corridor and gagged.

CHAPTER 70

"*I must say, you look stunning in that gown. Even better than you did through my* lens from atop that building." McKenzey stared at Kareem's dumbstruck face. The look was priceless. McKenzey grabbed his walkie-talkie cell phone and radioed for his colleagues, who were at the hospital cafeteria having breakfast. McKenzey stayed back to watch his prize, and he did not need breakfast. He was full of anticipation and hope.

Kareem was visibly torn. *How could Toi let this happen to me? She knew that this pussy was out here waiting for me!* In anger, he tried to lunge at McKenzey, who stepped aside swiftly, and caused Kareem to slam hard to the floor. Toi rushed to his aid.

"Careful. I'll hit a cripple."

"Fuck you." Kareem screamed, as Toi helped him up. "If you hurt my grandmother you asshole, I will kill you, I promise you that."

Nurses dashed down the corridor after hearing the commotion. One of them in teal scrubs told him, "Mr. Bezel, you need to be in bed resting. You're under strict doctor order, and you're scheduled for surgery. You need to rest."

Kareem was put back into his bed, and was fuming. His shooter was in the hospital room and was in full control. Kareem wanted to howl and transform into a werewolf. Where was Dre when he needed him? He had to get out of there. The way things looked, his only way out was to be admitted into the Metropolitan Detention Center in Brooklyn, New York.

With Kareem snuggled in his bed, three other agents rushed into his room. There was not anything more desperate than a bunch of incompetent agents abusing someone's Fourth Amendment right. He stared at the villainous agents—two men and a token woman—and realized that he may need to dig deep to fend off the unprincipled clan. Kareem was sure that McKenzey and company had carefully selected several crooked clones from a clever stock of agents, from which to take the Bezel's down. Kareem hoped that the other three was not as indecorous as McKenzey.

"You came all the way up to New York just to arrest lil' ol' moi?" Kareem asked with a mocking disbelief.

"Oh, Mr. Bezel. It'll be an honor to haul you off right now to MDC, but you're not under arrest," one of the agents said.

"Don't worry, you won't be going today, but I assure you faster than you can heal, your new doctor will be a Navy Reservist at the federal jail," Agent Melvin Tyler said.

"What a criminal bomb shell?" Kareem said, disgustedly and rolled his eyes to the back of his head. "I guess that I should raise the white flag and announce my cease fire."

"This is just the first of many cease fires," Agent Tyler told him. "We have investigations for embezzlement, drug trafficking…"

"Murder for hire, conspiracy," Agent Bollaski added.

"Credit card fraud, bank fraud, racketeering, you name it, we have you on it," Agent Tyler said.

"And I have a lawyer to get me off it," Kareem said calmingly. He had no idea if his next words would be effective, but he had to make them appear convincing. "Trust me on this, McKenzey, you'll regret shooting me."

"Kareem...Kareem...Kareem," McKenzey rambled shaking his head. "Are we going to go there, again? We've been over this once before, and trust me; you will not trigger an approved audit of my behaviors." The look on McKenzey's face was unconquerable, as he leaned over his once invincible foe and whispered, "By the way, thanks for the...uh...half million. I'm already looking for a new home in an expensive foreign zip."

Kareem opened his mouth to speak.

"Don't think of ever disrespecting my senior officer. If you weren't hurt, I'd be all over your scrawny ass myself," the sour-faced female Agent Small told him. "You're like an incurable disease."

"She speaks," Kareem said, grinning. He started to launch a verbal attack on her, but he was cut off again.

"Watch it, bitch!" Toi interjected. "Why the fuck your bull dagging ass keep cutting him off."

"Get her out of here," Agent Bollaki yelled wrathfully. Agent Tyler grabbed Toi by the arm and ushered her to the door.

"You can't kick me out. He is not under arrest. Get your hands off me you son-of-a-bitch." Toi screamed, and tried to resist his grip. "Kareem," she yelled. "I'm calling, Dre."

"Good. We've been looking for him."

Medical staff witnessed the commotion. "Okay guys, that is enough." The room door was being held open by a doctor who entered the room. With his soft mousey voice, he told the agents, "He needs to undergo surgery. You'll need to be gone before he returns, so that he can recover." The doctor checked the brake on the bed and prepared to sit his patient into the wheelchair.

"He's been receptive to our questions thus far," said McKenzey.

"Hell, we will be right here waiting for him to return," the female agent said. She had a lot of mouth and a nasty disposition.

"I'm sure that he has a conscious spirit. However, his arm and shoulder needs to be addressed and he does not need police anxiety as he recoups," the doctor said. "If you'd give him three days before you return that'll be great. Or, I could have a court order to blockade your access to him for a few months."

CHAPTER 71

"*Doc, where are we going?*" *Kareem asked. The elevator passed floors 4, 3, 2,* and headed towards the lobby. That alarmed Kareem. He had little knowledge of the hospital. Something was strangely wrong. His brain swirled with a rush of questions and concerns.

He remembered that before they entered the elevator, the doctor stopped anyone else from entering it. He then inserted a key into the elevator, preventing it from stopping at any other levels. Kareem was not happy with the doctor's doggerel.

The hospital elevator doors parted, and the wheelchair rolled out into the corridor. The sign plastered on the wall had an arrow pointing to the left. Next to the arrow were the words: LOBBY/EXIT. The wheelchair turned left. Kareem panicked. Never had a hospital corridor seemed so empty and quiet.

Kareem gathered his mettle, and said, "I have no idea what the fuck you're doing, but when we pass the lobby, I'll scream, if you don't tell me where we are going." Kareem was scared that he was being kidnapped by a McKenzey operative. He had a half-frown on his face.

"If you utter one word, we won't"—the doctor paused and removed the voice-changing device from his throat, then continued in his deeper, familiar tone—"we won't leave!"

"Marquis," Kareem whispered excitedly.

"Shhh! Damn, we have to make it to the exit before the agents decide to put a man on your operating room."

"How'd you pull this off?" Kareem asked. He was in utter disbelief.

"Your arm is fucked up, but is your brain dead?" Marquis asked, trivially, wheeling past the hospital reception area. He had the audacity to nod to security, and wished them a good morning.

They rolled right out the door to a line of cars parked to one side of the hospital. Marquis loaded Kareem into a red and black BMW Z3, under the pouring rain.

* * *

*T*oi could not believe what she had been told. The doctor took Kareem away. *What the fuck! Is that a joke?* She knew that McKenzey was responsible. He had sent a man to kidnap and torture Kareem. *What do I do now?* She ran behind the officers who drove away as she stood there on the pavement by herself, being rained on. She sobbed fiercely. *Where do I go?*

What would I do without Kareem? I'm having a baby, for Christ-sakes. Why did he have to do the things that he did? He's too smart for his own good. And everyone desires him to be my perfect man. I should have moved on. Wait! I tried that. He turned out to be an agent trying to get Kareem. Somebody help me!

Toi gathered her composure just as the hospital nurse in the teal scrub handed her a business envelope and walked away without a word. Toi was perplexed and opened the envelope eagerly. She walked away from the hospital and read the note. Midway through it, she smiled, folded it and moved into action.

CHAPTER 72

*S*peeding down Lexington Avenue, Marquis violated a host of traffic laws. He narrowly escaped a murder charge as a scantily clad woman carrying a Bloomingdale's shopping bag dove hard onto the curb. Cops and federal agents were in pursuit of the shrewd pair. McKenzey was obnoxiously impressed at the foxy gambit.

They had gotten more attention than necessary. Marquis' eyes stayed glued on the road. Kareem kept looking behind them. He had an unnecessary eye on their exposed pursuers.

Turning onto a one lane street, Kareem found them behind a UPS truck holding up traffic delivering a package. Kareem became frustrated. He looked behind them and saw a black sedan directly behind them. They couldn't back up. Nowhere to go. Nowhere to turn. Marquis turned to his pal and shrugged his shoulder as he turned the wheel, directing the car into the entrance of a parking garage.

"What the fuck are you doing?" Kareem asked his voice full of panic. "Take the curb!"

Marquis ignored his panic. He had things under control. The car spiraled to the top of the garage, and McKenzey slithered behind them. They crawled deeper into the garage and Kareem grew displeased with Marquis' actions.

The top level of the garage was empty, but there was nowhere to go. Kareem was pissed. "Why the fuck run, if you don't have a plan?" He screamed. He was so upset with Marquis for tobogganing them into another hostile conflict, while McKenzey having shot him was fresh.

D-Block's CD thumped in the background, creating a dangerous atmosphere. The police men sat forty-feet behind them in the otherwise empty top level of the garage. One of their voices came over a bullhorn filling the Z3. "Give it up boys. Turn the car engine off and place the car keys on the roof of the car."

Marquis turned down the music and Kareem said, "Now what, dickhead! I told you not to come in here. How many fucking times have you seen someone get away in this scenario?" He screamed in disgust. After all the work they had put in, they now faced arrest, or death. And worse, he had no idea where Jean-Mary was. Kareem wanted to beat Marquis the fuck up.

Marquis was placid, though. "Kareem you've always led the way. You have no idea how much I respect you, applaud you—"

"Gentleman! This is DEA Agent Lucas McKenzey. I implore you to step out of the vehicle with our hands up. You have families. Please do not make any false moves. I'd hate to see this turned into news."

Marquis ignored the agent and continued to praise his best friend. "Despite being older than you, I envy you, and equally respect you. And maybe, I'm even a little jealous.

Most importantly, I love you, dawg." Marquis pause and looked ahead of them, then back at Kareem. He again looked ahead, and then back at Kareem.

Kareem caught on and couldn't believe his eyes. "Why the fuck not?"

CHAPTER 73

*T*he BMW-Z3 roared across the garage, reaching fifty miles per hour. It crashed through the weak barrier and soared through the air. Marquis was glad that he was able to hit the barrier at the precise point that he had rigged. They floated three seconds, six-feet across an alley before the car plowed into the neighboring garage.

"Un-fucking-believable," McKenzey said crazily as he pulled his hair and looked in amazement. He grabbed the walkie-talkie from the NYPD officer that was closes to him and radioed the back up cars. He alerted them that the fugitives were in the opposite garage. "Cut him off." He yelled, turning his car around.

"We're entering the garage now. They're not going anywhere, I promise you that," one of the NYPD cars responded with confidence.

"Proceed with caution. They may be armed and dangerous," McKenzey said, with a visual of BG and Avery on his mind.

* * *

"What the fuck do you mean you can't find them?" McKenzey ranted to NYPD officer Javier Adderly, the first officer on the scene.

Ten officers ran wildly through the garage trying to locate the fugitives. Three minutes had passed, and they were nowhere to be found. Neither was the Z3.

"They vanished, sir," Adderly screamed into his walkie-talkie. His stiff gelled crew cut was limp from sweat.

"That's impossible. Z3's don't fucking vanish. Check every car, inside and underneath. Force every driver to lift their hood and open their trunk. No one leaves even if they are clean. Interview everyone."

McKenzey parked his cruiser. He jumped out and greeted NYPD Sergeant Wu. "I need your men to search every car. These two cannot leave this garage. Have them take posts around the perimeter. And for a few blocks until I get the tunnels and bridges closed. Nothing leaves out of Manhattan."

The cops searched feverishly, car by car, and stopped every car owner. McKenzey had no idea where they hid, but he was sure that they could not have left the garage. They had to be in someone's car, but where was the Z3. They checked every stairwell, in the cash booth, and atop the elevators. There was no sign of them. To make matters worse, McKenzey had no idea who the doctor was. Who tipped the impersonator to rescue Kareem? Where was Dre? His mind raced uncontrollably.

"Attention. I have two silhouettes under a blue sedan. Looks like a Camry. I'm approaching it, with caution," Officer Adderly said.

"Where are you?" McKenzey asked.

"Level 3." Officer Adderly had his arms fully extended, as his right hand held gripped his left wrist for a steady shot. He approached the car when one of the figures twitched. He panicked and yelled, "Freeze. Don't move." *Dear God, please do not let them move.*

Other officers and McKenzey arrived on the third level ready to go. They were all cautious, though. McKenzey knew all to well that Kareem was full of surprises and he would put nothing past him. Even though Adderly had controlled the scene, McKenzey took charge.

"Look, Kareem. It's over. There's two dozen police, that's 24 guns out here. Do you want that to mean anything? Come on, pal. Do it for Jean-Mary."

"We give up and are going to come out. Don't kill us," a voice screamed out from under the car.

"Okay boys. Any tricks and you will lose. The odds are seriously stacked against you," McKenzey assured his suspects.

The NYPD and DEA agents took over, positioned throughout the garage to avoid a sniper-style truce.

Sgt. Wu screamed out, "One of you crawl out now and remain faced down."

A lanky figure snaked from under the Camry. He laid face down in the middle of the driveway. McKenzey was impressed that they had changed from their hospital garments so quickly. He liked that they were determined to persevere.

"Okay. Now you, number two. Same thing, crawling, remember. No sudden movements, and faced down."

He too complied.

"One of guys is going to come and cuff you two. He'll be unarmed, so do not think about grabbing his weapon."

Three men approached the pair. One had his gun drawn and the other two cuffed the men. That went smoothly. With the men hand cuffed, McKenzey and company rolled up on them and pulled them to their feet. McKenzey was flabbergasted as he looked at two teenaged boys, not Kareem and his unidentified perp.

"Why the hell are you under a car?" McKenzey asked furiously. He would have killed them if he were alone.

"We thought that you were looking for us because we ran away from home," a thirteen-year-old said, shaking his head, scared of all the guns drawn on him.

"Did you see a BMW Z3? Red?" McKenzey asked.

"Yes! I saw the driver toss a mask over there," one of the boys said pointing.

"Yeah, the car rolled up into the cargo area of a UPS truck, like Kit from Knight Rider."

CHAPTER 74

*T*he Elmhurst section of Queens was filled to the brim with NYPD, DEA, and the FBI. McKenzey stood behind the barrier surrounding a UPS truck. Even though the truck appeared empty, McKenzey warned the officers not to approach the vehicle until the bomb squad had cleared the area for police scrutiny. Channel-9 news circled the scene from the air for an exclusive shot of the proceedings.

McKenzey looked on as the FBI Special Agent Assistant Director in charge of the New York office approached the scene. The Bezels had made capturing them course enough, but this stunt was vulgar and needed the attention of the big wigs. Director Mason Dillard was a slim, morbid-looking man. The bespectacled agent approached McKenzey, who realized he was about to receive one of the most daunting humiliations a cop could get: a reprimand from the top brass.

The Bezels had truly strengthened McKenzey's loathsome opinion of them. He should have taken then down, rather than allow them to obscenely exploit the agency for its incompetence.

Dilliard stood face-to-face with McKenzey. He removed his glasses and stared down the subordinate. "Right now, I know you're shitting in your pants. Hating their ferocious punch of perseverance and determination to hold onto their freedom another day. I bet you're as amazed as I am at how they have an aggressive skill in coaxing your egoism. Your bullshit—which, I have saw tapes—has drained the morals and righteousness and nobility out of the agency's existence."

"Sir, with all—"

"I urge not to speak. Anything you say just may eventually be used against you. Capturing these clowns is the only language that I'd like to hear from you. And I never want you in my fucking city again!" Dilliard paused and took a deep breath, staring hard into McKenzey's eyes. "I hope you understand that my last name is not Bezel," he said and walked away.

McKenzey watched Dilliard's back and wanted to shoot a bullet through it. McKenzey felt the dark glare's from his team. They wondered if there was any ethical coherence in McKenzey's blood. All of Kareem's words—"he shot me"—and Dilliard's words—"I've seen the tapes"—flashed through their minds.

The bomb squad robot rolled away from the truck, a cold wind of thoughts battered McKenzey's mind, frustrating him. The robot could not have departed an instant too soon. The amount of dreadful suspense turned out to be the most excruciating moment of his life. The robot's intelligence revealed that the truck was clean. Agents surrounded the trucks with their guns drawn as McKenzey raised the cargo door of the truck nearest him. There was a note hanging on the back wall of the truck, along with a laptop. The note read: *So long sucka. See you in Mexico!*

Suddenly the idea of them being at the airport dawned on the cops, and that was a hazard. McKenzey looked at Sgt. Wu and raced off to his car. McKenzey's task force followed their leader to the airport.

* * *

Sgt. Wu stayed at the crime scene to see to it that things went accordingly. The remaining NYPD snatched up the laptop and opened it. It was a showing of the local channel-9 news. They looked at the 20-inch screen in disbelief.

"This is a special news bulletin, live on WXRP channel-9 news," the news announcer said over the breaking news music.

Christina Marx peered into camera "A," her gold locks and red-orange lipstick, complimented her orange business suit jacket. She read the breaking news from the TelePrompter.

"Sorry to interrupt your programming, but we have breaking news. A police chase ended this morning after new fashion designer, Bjorne Prodigy, born Kareem Bezel, craftily escaped arrest at a local hospital." She paused as the screen flashed to the news helicopter that hovered over the Queens parking lot, where Sgt. Wu and his team watched themselves on the lap top.

Christina Marx continued, "The chase began when Agent Lucas McKenzey from the Philadelphia DEA's office and his task force enlisted the New York office to assist with taking down the future mogul for a laundry list of crimes. Here is Daniel Moore from our Philadelphia affiliate with more."

"That's right, Christina. Kareem Bezel, noted for his upscale new fashion line has been implicated as the king pin of a drug ring, rumored to have supplied Philadelphia and the suburbs with kilos of cocaine over the last four years. However, I have right here"—he paused and theatrically waved a tape in the air—"evidence proving that a decorated DEA agent supplied him with the drugs and money, and forced him and his brother to sell for him against their will. If they did not comply, McKenzey threatened to make them disappear, as he did their father who has been in federal jail and presently pending appeal. To run this ring, McKenzey has spiked the cocaine of a drug abusing councilman, who demanded more money in exchange for information regarding local authorities' efforts to bring down McKenzey's number one supplier, Brent Gower, a local thug who died a terrible death at the hands of McKenzey. McKenzey gunned down another drug dealer, Avery Snobli. This tape shows McKenzey tampering with the dead body to make it appear like a robbery, which he later attempted to blame on Andre Bezel. Agent Turner, whose home was blown up with his wife and children inside, were killed by McKenzey, after he found that the brother's had black mailed Turner to hand over all of the investigative notes that he had as he posed undercover as a potential boy toy of Kareem's fiancé.

Agent Turner also recorded a tape indicating that McKenzey had doctored investigative material to implicate the brothers. Lastly, Agent Belton of Internal Affairs was murdered at his New Jersey home, when McKenzey learned that he had found all the evidence on this tape to take McKenzey off the streets. Note that the Bezel's grandmother, Jean-Mary Bezel, age 73 has disappeared and McKenzey is a prime suspect in her disappearance. Stay tuned for my complete exposé."

The feed switched back to Christina Marx taking a signal for going off the air. She signed off.

* * *

With the broadcast over, Christina went into her dressing room and dialed her cell phone. She spoke into it, "We're off the air and agents are scampering from the UPS truck now. Our helicopters are on them, so I'll give you a play-by-play account of their moves."

"Ok, good. We're crossing the George Washington Bridge into Jersey now," Marquis told her.

CHAPTER 75

There was panic in the airport. *Men and women in suits raced around, searching* for the Bezel party. They checked everyone who fit their characteristics. The Patriot Act allowed them to violate everyone's privacy at the airport without question.

McKenzey screamed at a travel agent. "Check your manifest for any passengers with the last name, Bezel."

The frightened agent blew her hair from her forehead and typed fast on her keyboard. "There's four here, sir," she said. "But that flight left twenty minutes ago."

The flight was ordered back to JFK and was secured at the terminal. The FBI agents, headed by McKenzey, clogged the jet-way connected to the plane. The plane door opened and McKenzey sped past the flight attendant. Guns drawn, he and his colleagues searched every passenger. Row-by-row, they checked, double-checked, and triple-checked for the Bezel clan. There was no sign of them.

Panic, fear, hatred, defeat all consumed McKenzey. That was not happening. They had to be there. Frustrated, McKenzey ran back to the airline check-in counter.

Agent Dilliard told him, "It's over, McKenzey. Give it up. Let's end this quietly."

McKenzey looked at them with a puzzled expression, as he swiftly grabbed an agent by the neck. He snuggled his bicep around her throat, restricting her air passage.

"You are in an airport, in New York City, home of Ground Zero. One false move and every civilian in here will attack you. You can't leave, and you're out gunned."

McKenzey used his free hand to grab his gun from his waist. He stuffed the barrel of the Calico into the temple of his hostage. She began to sob and shake, and he tightened his grip. He stared at Dilliard and every agent felt his hate. They feared his next move would leave a few dead men in the airport.

"That's a beautiful toy, you have there. I doubt that is bureau issued?" Dilliard asked.

"Did you think that my arrest would be easy? Whoever gave you this order undoubtedly briefed you on my skill. I bet they swore to you that they had me all figured out, didn't they? Now look, I have a hostage to get out of here. Doesn't that make you ponder their ability to lead? You stick to protocol, and let me out of here. Remember the rules of a hostage situation?" McKenzey asked tauntingly.

Dilliard knew the rules, but he also knew that the hostage would be dead if he did not save her from McKenzey's grip. "Let the girl go, McKenzey," Dilliard said frankly. "You'll never get away. You're no longer an agent. As of this moment you're suspended of your duties. Hand over your badge and gun. That's a direct order from the White House."

"Does that mean that I am a civilian, again? You or those chumps in Washington, you know, the people that are playing your tunes, can't stop me."

"It's true, McKenzey. I'm a piano. George Bush is playing the keys, and if you listen closely, you can hear the fat lady singing."

"Sir, permission to shoot, sir?" Agent Tyler yelled, with a direct shot of McKenzey.

"Go ahead, Agent Tyler, kill me. They'll just go on to exploit you and the rest of you fools'." McKenzey said, and let out a sinister laugh. McKenzey's head throbbed badly. His face was molten with hatred. He wanted to smash his victim's face. He envisioned cracking her neck, and after that Dilliard's too.

An agent lost control.

A shot was fired.

EPILOGUE

(SIX DAYS LATER)

CHAPTER 76

While McKenzey's hand had been severely damaged it remained attached to his wrist in a hard cast. Probably, he would never gain a feeling in it, or use it too pull the trigger needed to gain revenge on the Bezel brother's. He looked forward to learning to masturbate with his left hand, though. He remained hopeful that Belton would get him out of his quandary.

One of his own men, the cocky Agent Small had shot him in the hand. What a shooter she was. And expertly, as she did not harm the hostage.

"McKenzey yard?" a correctional officer at the Federal Detention Center-Philadelphia asked through the locked cell door.

McKenzey was being held pending a bail hearing, and was in the Special Housing Unit on the 8th floor for his own protection. The way he saw it, the other inmates were being sheltered from his years in combat. He wanted to kick some ass.

"Fuck you, asshole! I'm not going into that cage like an animal. Take your mother to the yard." He barked angrily at the CO. "Yeah, your mother!"

"You're such an animal, you may as well go out and get some sun," the CO replied. "You're never going home, so hey, why not get use to this before you're off to Big Sandy, because I assure you that you will be serving this entire bid in PC." The CO was very calm, and strolled away from the cell, leaving McKenzey kicking violently on the door.

CHAPTER 77

A short week had passed almost to the day of his grand escape, and Kareem was at the bargaining table. He sat in an office at the United States District Attorney's Office, between 6th and 7th Streets on Chestnut in downtown Philadelphia. He wanted to toss Barnswell from that 6th floor window, and really show him who was in charge. He sat at the round table with Ravonne Lemmelle by his side. A lone FBI Agent was in the room presumably as a spectator, as he hadn't opened his mouth through the entire deposition. The questions were clear and direct. And the outcome was simple.

"So," Barnswell said. "I read your statement and I must say that it reeks of fiction, but your hard evidence is hard to contradict. It's going to be a task to convince my superiors to go for you being an un-indicted co-conspirator without you getting on the witness stand."

"I don't do boxes."

"Kareem!" Lemmelle chided. "You listen, and I speak. Go on Barnswell."

"Sounds fair," Barnswell said with a sneer on his ugly face. "I'm going to run this by them, but I want Andre Bezel at that marshal's office by three p.m. today, or this whole chicanery is off."

"Off as it relates to Andre?" Lemmelle asked. He wanted to be clear. "That is not my client, and his decisions do not affect mine."

"Technically, they don't, but surely that deal plays a part in this one. I can't believe I have softened to this."

"Of course you do. He, Agent McKenzey, that is, forced these young men to sell his drugs and he molested them when they were younger, while he sold drugs with their father. And because his father attempted to kill him for it, he had the man locked away. You're doing the right thing here, Barnswell." Lemmelle couldn't believe that he let that bullshit come out of his Harvard mouth. He was a sworn officer of the court, but he was equally a member of the National Attorney's Lying Society. The members met regularly in courtrooms across America.

"And you say Jean-Mary is where?" Barnswell asked.

"Safe, but traumatized by the whole being bound to the bed thing. Speaking of which, is Belton being punished for her kidnapping?" said Lemmelle.

"He has been charged, but remember that we cut a deal for him to disclose her location. I think we're done here. Remember Kareem, do not leave the city of Philadelphia."

"About that," Kareem said, calmly. "You know that I live in New York City."

"No…You live in Philadelphia. I've left enough of your money unfrozen for you to get a place. I don't care if you sleep at 30th Street Station, I seriously advise you not to leave. That will breach your contract with my office, and I assure you that you'll get 30-years easily, and Lemmelle won't be able to stop it!" He paused at shot Lemmelle a look that dared him to defy his words. "Is there anything else?"

"No," That was Lemmelle.

"Yes," Kareem said, quickly. "My father, what's being done to have him released?"

"Nothing!"

"Pardon me. You know that he is innocent."

"Come on, Lemmelle. Didn't you teach him that there are many innocent men in prison? A victim of their circumstance. Likewise, there are men guilty as all hell walking around the streets ready for their next lick, because they were released for some technical legal precedent. You're father know his remedies, but, uh, no, I won't be assisting with his release." *How could I,* Barnswell thought. *After all, I helped McKenzey put him there, and I am going to get you too, buddy.* "Tell your dad, I wish him the best. Have a nice day, Mr. Bezel."

If you thought LAUGH NOW was a thrill, and desire more of Rahiem Brooks, its coming soon.

Please turn this page to get a conniving filled peek at

CON TEST

a Prodigy Publishing Group, hardcover coming soon.

Prologue

MEET JUSTICE LORENZO

One

The Wachovia Bank teller had no idea that she would be robbed that day. Had she known, perhaps she may not have reported for duty. She would not experience an ordinary robbery, though. Not one involving drawn guns or threatening notes. Her life would not be in jeopardy. Nor would she witness a sophisticated scheme to drill through the bank's vault. That robbery would be deceitful and conniving, but as devastating in its effect as any armed caper.

Wachovia Bank customer, Lervern Grisby, had parked in the bank's parking lot. The shadows from the pine trees neatly lined across the back of the lot forced the warm autumn air to seem chilly. Lervern checked her garish make-up in the rearview mirror, before she opened the car door. She quivered as an eerie chill came over her. She walked slowly and apprehensively from the handicapped parking space. She was a jazzy black woman, clad in daywear and donned a cane.

She approached the bank door. Before she reached out to open it, the door swung open. A security guard held the door open until she crossed the threshold. That was why she adored Wachovia: extraordinary customer relations from the moment customers were on the property. She flashed him a prismatic smile, and showcased teeth that were so perfectly capped that they were enviable. She thanked him and gleefully waltzed across the dark green carpet.

Although Lervern peered over her shoulder from time to time expecting a black, derelict, thug brandishing a gun, or worse, a white man with a bomb foolishly wrapped snuggly about his throat to rush into the bank behind her, she fell in line behind three other customers. She prayed the bad men were on hiatus that morning.

Lervern stood in the roped line and used her cane as an additional leg. She rested her hand on the chrome post; it was cool. She was hot, though. She pulled a church fan from her Chanel handbag and began to fan herself. The air hit her nostrils, and she smelled potpourri, which sat in bowls all around the bank. She hoped that her allergies did not act up. If so, she would sweat and have a sneezing attack. Either would ruin her make-up, and ultimately her day.

She turned her head to look around the bank and her large, gray curls swung wildly. Along the wall behind her were three customer service representatives chatting with customers. To the left of them was the vault complete with an armed sentry. Lervern glanced at her watch and then was instructed by a white flashing arrow to proceed to the available teller.

In front of the teller, she removed extra-large Fendi glasses and slipped them into her bag. She used a gloved hand and a fancy pen to sign a withdrawal slip.

"How may I help you today?" the teller asked smiling.

"A withdrawal, sweetie," Lervern said, and stacked above that she said, "Here's a withdrawal slip from the back of my checkbook. I have signed the slip, but with my arthritis,"—she held up a mildly shaking writing hand—"Could you? Would you mind filling out the remainder of the slip?" She pleaded in her raspy, deep, southern drawl.

The teller looked at the elderly woman, and said, "Of course not, ma'am. I have your account number here on the bottom of the slip. All I need is the amount you'd like to withdraw, and see photo identification along with a second form of ID."

"Oh, certainly," Lervern said, pulling out her wallet to retrieve her ID. "I need a cashiers check for…Shoot," Lervern said, frustratingly, as she passed the teller her ID. She took a deep breath and then coughed into a cupped hand over her mouth. "Pardon me," she said, apologetically.

"Its okay, Ms. Grisby," the teller cooed. "Take your time," she told her. "Can I get you a cup of water?"

"No…no. I'll be fine. Thanks, though," Lervern said, having gathered her composure. "Math has never been my strongest subject. Could you tally two months rent and two months security, if the rent is $1,400 per month. I'll need a check for that amount. Also, $3,000 in cash. Could you add that accordingly for me, please?"

"Sure, no problem."

"You're a doll."

"A $5,600 cashier's check and $3,000 in cash will be a total withdrawal of $8,600," the teller said, filling out the withdrawal slip as she spoke. She then handed the slip to Lervern. "Verify the amount for me, Ms. Grisby and place your right thumb print on the slip, as well. Thanks."

Lervern scanned the slip and handed it back to the teller without the thumb print. "Hun, these protective arthritis gloves are a pain to get off, and worse to squeeze on. My hands swell, and…"

The teller cut her off, politely. "But—"

Ms. Grisby returned the favor. "I have not been here in a while, but the head teller over there"—she pointed to a white woman whom scanned a spreadsheet—"could verify who I am," she said. "She used to help me when I came in daily to make business deposits."

"You mean Rose Daniels. She's the head teller. Let me get her," the teller said, stepping away from her station. She showed Rose the withdrawal slip and two pieces of identification and informed her of the situation.

Both women walked back over to Lervern.

"How've you been, Ms. Grisby?" Rose asked, sincerely.

"I'm fine. This arthritis acts a fool, but otherwise, I'm sixty-six-years-young. And you?"

"Peachy! Its been some time since you last visited us, huh? How's the business heading up?" Rose asked, throwing Lervern a smile.

"Business is fine. The children are running it since I've retired," Lervern said. She switched gears to get the topic off her. "You've moved up, I see. Congrats!"

"Thanks...Ms. Grisby, I do not mean to cut this short, but I have a budget due in half-an-hour. Just jot your birth date and social security number down on the withdrawal slip, and I will approve your transaction. Thanks."

Lervern gave the back of her fan a quick glance for her personal data. She knew the information, but liked to be careful. She complied with Rose's request and watched the bankers verify the information on the computer monitor. Rose initialed the slip, offered Lervern a good day, and sent the teller to fabricate the cashier's check.

Lervern watched the teller, as her pulse began to march double time. A hot ball of acid, scorching and burning, elevated from her stomach to her chest. Lervern suddenly felt that she was trapped in a vat of hot air. She fanned herself before she had a panic attack. She kept her ears alert, head held high. Lervern was not prepared for another dangerous bank episode.

Four minutes passed and the teller came back with the check. She punched buttons on her computer keyboard, and then counted $3,000 from her drawer. She placed the notes into an envelop and then handed it to her customer. Lervern counted the bills and then tucked the envelop into her bosom.

"Can I do anything else for you, ma'am?"

"Just a receipt with the balance, and I'll be outta your hair."

"Sure. Let me get your receipt, and—"

The teller was interrupted by loud music, which blared from a cell phone. With the phone out of Lervern's bag, the teller and Lervern distinctly heard the chorus to the Ying Yang Twins *Whisper* song: *Wait till you see my dick.* Both the teller and Lervern gagged.

Lervern spoke into the phone: "Before you ask, yes, I found your phone in my car. I had planned on dropping it to you with the check for your rent deposit and money for college. That was before I heard this ring-tone...Sorry, nothing...Do you know how embarrassing this is, I'm still in the bank, boy...I don't want to hear it...Is that what you play to those young gals you're having sex with, 'cause I have seen it, and it ain't worth waiting to see...Sure it grew, tell me anything!" Ms. Grisby slammed the phone shut and turned her attention back to the teller.

"That's right. You tell him grandma," the teller joked. She handed Lervern the receipt and asked, "Will that be all?"

"Yes, and have a nice day," Lervern said, and then left the bank.

* * *

3

Lervern reached her car, tossed her cane into the back seat, and sat slowly in the driver's seat. She started the ignition and backed out of the parking space. She eased her Prada Mary Jane's down on the accelerator and blended with the two-lane Cheltenham Avenue traffic. Her heart pounded. She adjusted the ventilation to a cool sixty-five degrees. She needed to cool and calm down. She had survived. She glanced into her mirror slightly disoriented, as she drove away from the bank into a morning so brilliant and indigo and full of hope for the future.

With all intent on getting away from the bank, she drove hastily west on the avenue, like a bat out of hell. Certainly, not like an elderly woman. She turned southbound onto Broad Street, and shortly thereafter, she flipped a left onto a small street. Her only purpose for that turn was to ditch the stolen vehicle that she had been driving. She put the car in park, and turned her fake grandson's cell phone back on. She dialed a friend who answered on the second ring.

"What's crackin'?" Flocco, the Puerto Rican chop-shop runner asked.

"This is JL, I have something for you," Justice Lorenzo said in his authentic, late night, radio-type voice.

"Yeah!" Flocco responded, excitedly. He knew that Justice was good for new vehicles.

"I am stepping out of a Nissan Maxima with 683 miles, straight from Enterprise." Justice confessed, stepping femininely out of the Maxima remaining in character. He hopped into a navy Cadillac Escalade.

"I need dat. What color?"

"Metallic gold."

"Good...Good. Six-thousand, right?"

"Homey," Justice said, disgustedly. "A brand new wheel. Don't try to play me, nigga. I need ten, or I go to the New Yorkers." There were no New Yorkers, but Flocco did not know that, though.

"Man, ten is steep. I tell you what—"

Justice interrupted him. "Ten, Flocco!"

"Aiight, pa, damn. I'll pick up the keys and bring the cash later tonight."

* * *

Justice drove back out onto Broad Street, then continued west on the county dividing, Cheltenham Avenue. On the right side of the avenue—the side that he meandered along—was Montgomery County. The world was deepening into the new century. Just when he had lost faith in the idea of fulfilling an American dream and mentally extinguishing his aspirations, he found the courage to rise from amongst the dead. His bottomless well of ideas burned bright, and on that beautiful autumn morning he promised to attain the ultimate goal of all: becoming a celebrity.

Cruising along the crowded avenue, he brood whether his family would find the same faith in him. He had become the biggest Lorenzo Family fuck up. He was morbidly determined to lose that crown, though. He lowered the system and dialed his friend, Amiriano, whom answered on the first ring.

"My nigga, what was all that bullshit you said to me, when I called a few minutes ago."

4

"I left my cell phone on, and I had to improvise," Justice told him.

Amiriano let out a brief gasp. He could not believe that Justice could be so erroneous. Since Justice had retired, Amiriano had been his only thief-in-training. "So, the Twins was banging all in the bank?" Amiriano asked, laughing.

"Man, that shit was scary and funny. That's what I be tryinna show you. You gotta be ready for anything. I kept thinking that them alphabet boys was going to run up in there. The same bitch that testified at my trial handled my transaction."

"Wow, that's crazy. You're back out and back at it, and got the bitch that had you booked. You're a bold nigga. Them boys was not going to run up in there on Ms. Lervern Grisby," Amiriano said, chuckling. Everything was comical to him with this game.

"I'm tryinna get this bitch bagged and tagged and burned, fo' real, homey," Justice said, unbuttoning a few buttons on his blouse. No one could see through his tinted windows. "This old lady has to go."

"They're not going to link you to this shit later, are they?"

"Naw. The teller filled out the slip and I did not leave a thumb print. So, no handwriting or finger print analysis."

"And definitely, no video would ID you. You did a great job."

"Yeah! I am the teacher remember?"

"I remember. What you got planned today?"

"Gotta run this crash dummy I met last week to the bank to cash this cashiers check. Then I am going to meet M&M. And after that, I have a class: Forensic Science."

"You swear you're a smart nigga. Forensic Science."

"That's how I'mma beat 'em, and get revenge. We are working on finding evidence on bodies today."

"That's crazy. Holla at a nigga when you leave M&M's," Amiriano said and hung up.

Justice drove and had pondered, even if he did build a conglomerate that secured a lion share of the urban fiction industry, married and lived on an estate as big as Oprah's, would his mother accept his success, knowing that the seed money was illegally gained? He glanced up and saw Cheltenham Square Mall on his right. He turned left onto Washington Lane and ultimately back into Philadelphia County.

A few streets away he turned onto the manicured lawn, tree lined, Briar Road. He pulled into the driveway and parked in his aunt's garage. Safely in the garage the large door quietly closed behind him. The adrenaline rush had subdued, as he sat in the truck and peacefully contemplated his next job. *Bad Justice*, he thought. *Bad, bad Justice.*

He peered into the rearview mirror. Lervern Grisby smiled back at him. She was proud of him. He thanked her and walked from the garage into his basement lair. Justice was back.

Well, after he murdered, Ms. Lervern Grisby.

ABOUT RAHIEM BROOKS

Rahiem J. Brooks is the breakout urban thrill novelist with an overflowing reservoir of criminal tales that motivate American denizen to hug their purses and wallets. His tales prompt you to be overprotective of your sensitive personal data. After serving two relatively short federal white-collar prison terms of imprisonment, he is ready to show what white-collar crime in the hood is all about, as opposed to the billionaire unbelievable Hollywood crimes. He contributes seminars and commentary, as well as, works as a free-lance fraud prevention specialist for a range of companies and media outlets. He is a free-lance writer for Oak Lane Magazine, a Philadelphia based periodical. He studied film/TV at University of California, Los Angeles. He currently lives in Philadelphia, Pennsylvania branding his Prodigy Publishing Group.

Visit: www.rahiembrooks.com or www.facebook.com/rahiembrooks to find out when Rahiem will be on your block, pushing books and his message.

5296577R0

Made in the USA
Charleston, SC
25 May 2010